# JACK
# THE DEVIL'S PURSE

# JACK AND THE DEVIL'S PURSE

*Scottish Traveller Tales*

## Duncan Williamson
### Edited by Linda Williamson

BIRLINN

First published in 2011 by
Birlinn Limited
West Newington House
10 Newington Road
Edinburgh
EH9 1QS

*www.birlinn.co.uk*

ISBN: 978 1 84158 951 0

British Library Cataloguing-in-Publication Data
A catalogue record for this book is available from the British Library

Typeset by Hewer Text (UK) Ltd, Edinburgh
Printed and bound by Cox & Wyman, Reading

*To Donald*

# Contents

# Introduction

## The Coming of the Devil on Earth

According to the mythology of the Travelling People, God created Hell just the way He created Heaven. It was all over a simple argument. When God created all the Earth and everything else, He had many angels, people in Heaven to help him. And one that He liked more than anybody else was Lucifer; He loved Lucifer. And this angel looked up to God and adored everything that He did under the sun. Anything that God would do, Lucifer was always there. He was God's right-hand man in Heaven. But Lucifer had a mother, Magog, and he lived with her.

Now Magog loved her son dearly; he was her only son. But they were very unhappy, especially the old mother, because Magog believed her son was more powerful than God, and cleverer. She was jealous of her son's love for God.

She was always getting on to him and telling him, 'Why do you have to be at God's beck and call every moment? Why do you look up to this man and do everything for him? Why should he be the boss? You're as good as what he is. *You* could be that person instead of him! You're stronger than him; you're as clever as what he is.'

And this began to penetrate Lucifer's mind. He was a clever man. He was intelligent, had learned many things from God. So after his mother's aggravation for many nights, many weeks and many months he could stand it no more. He went to God and he tellt God all this that his mother had told him.

He said to God, 'Why do I need to bow before you? Am I just something you've created, that you can treat as a slave?'

And God said, 'No, you are my right-hand man. You're one of my favourites.'

Lucifer stood before God, 'Look, I'm just as powerful as you,' he said. 'I could be a king, King of the World – as what you are.'

God shook his head sadly. He said to Lucifer, 'By the way you talk and the way you think, I don't think you're qualified to take my place.'

But Lucifer said, 'I'm stronger and fitter than you, I'm more powerful! I'm stronger than any animal you've ever created on the Earth, this place you call Earth. I'm stronger than the wildest bull you've ever created.'

And God said, 'Well you don't look like one, but if you want to look like one . . .' and he pointed his finger like *that* – Lucifer felt a shudder going through him – he looked down. There he had a cloven hoof.

And he said, 'Why don't you make me king, why don't you make me Under-king?'

And God said to him, 'You want to be Under-king? In Heaven or Earth?'

And Lucifer says, 'I want to be King of Earth.'

God said, 'Well, I don't think I could make you King of Earth, because I already have plans for another king for Earth. But I can make you king – Under the Earth. You can rule Under the Earth for as long as you like, till the end of eternity.'

And there God created Hell. He sent Lucifer as a fallen angel to Under the Earth. And, of course, when Lucifer went, he took his mother with him.

The cavern of Hell with a burning fire to keep him company and no friends but his mother around made Lucifer very, very wicked. His name was then lost because he became the Prince of Darkness. He swore to his own mind that when anyone ever went into Earth, or was buried under the ground, even though they were dead he would take them and torment them for evermore. He was *evil*. And this word became 'devil', what he is called to this day, 'the Devil in Hell'.

Down through the centuries people of the world have come to call the Devil by many different names. No one wants to actually say *devil* because the word is too evil. They refer to him using by-names instead. In Scotland he is known as Old Hornie, because folk believe he has horns on his head; Old Clootie because he sometimes takes the place of a wreft or a spirit standing by the graveyard with a shroud over himself scaring people to death to get their souls; The Blacksmith because his place is beside his fire; and Old Rouchie because of his tough character. 'Cog' is the Travellers' word for him, referring to his art of deception and trickery.

To this day Travellers believe the Devil cannot show his face in daylight. And when he comes to you he appears in the form of a black dog, a black bull, a black stallion or in the form of a tall dark man. At night Cog can take his original form, for he is natural in darkness.

According to the Travellers' idea, the Devil does not exist in this world to get you and punish you and torture you for doing evil things. The Devil is there to outwit you! The idea goes back to when he tellt God, 'I'm more clever than you.'

When he was put to Hell he still maintained that. His wish was that he wanted to be King on Earth, so he comes to people on Earth to show he is superior – he wants to show he is cleverer than the people God has put on Earth. He gives them many chances to compete against him, 'Can you do something I can't do?'

If a person is clever enough to outwit the Devil then he leaves them in peace for evermore. But if they lose, their soul is lost and taken for torture in Hell. The saying 'May the Devil walk behind ye!' means 'may the Devil never catch up with you', or, may you always be one step ahead of him (evil) in the contest of intelligence and knowledge. When you come in contact with the Devil, and he comes to everyone, may you be cleverer than him and outdo the Enemy!

The point of the Devil stories is that every person has got an evil bit in him, let it be a child to a grown man, a girl to a grown woman. But it's only at a certain time that that piece of evil will ever show itself. Lucifer was evil when he went before God and challenged him. And God was upset. God knew that even though he was being evil there was something good in him forbyes. Because there's no such thing as an evil person through and through. Even the Devil is likeable. There's something good in every evil one and there's something evil in every good one. It's the balance between good and evil that makes for life on Earth. And this Earth wouldna be worth a-living on if it wasna for the Devil!

## The Night of the Circle

Hallowe'en, the 31st of October, is the night the Devil gets loose. It is his special night of freedom, when he and all the imps leave Hell, come and spread out through all the country. This belief goes back thousands of years in Scotland, when Hallowe'en was a night of wild festivity marking the end of the year for tribes of people known as the Celts. All year round they were hard-working, busy like ants or bees in a hive during the summer, getting things together to see them through the winter. Then on the eve of the Celtic New Year everything was let loose – people really did wicked things, things they would never do the rest of the year. They would exchange wives; they would get drunk, they would swear, they would curse. Nothing was sacred and no hold was barred. Every rule in the world was broken for a week or two weeks over the Hallowe'en festival. The Travellers believed the Devil was in the people at that time of year; they became devils.

Some would say, 'If you werena workin' with the Devil you wouldna do these things!'

At the centre of the Hallowe'en festival, even today, is the idea that the Devil is not to be clearly seen. Children dress up and put on 'false faces' at Hallowe'en just like the pagans did during their festival when the Devil came. He could walk among them and no one could distinguish him from the rest.

In my childhood times in Argyllshire, our Hallowe'en party was a wonderful night for us. We were tinkers, we'd never been invited inside the villagers' houses and never knew what it was like inside them – till Hallowe'en. But all the boys and girls of the village, me, my brothers and sisters dressed ourselves up trying to prove to everyone that nobody would find out who we really were. We would get old jackets or old coats, turn them inside out, blacken wir faces with coal cinders and get some sheep's wool to make a moustache or something. We would go round all the doors, each house in turn and knock 'chap chap'.

'Who is it?' they would say.

'Guisers – this is Hallowe'en night! Can we come in? What have you got for us?'

Oh, they'd take us into their house and give us something, a penny and a handful of nuts. But you had to sing a song!

Well, we would sing a song and then they'd say, 'Who are ye? Are ye one of Betsy's boys?' That was my mother, they knew my mother well.

'No,' we'd say, 'we're no one o' Betsy's boys.' You didna let them know who you were! But we'd tell them before we'd go on to the next house.

Then you had to duck for apples on the floor in a big bath. Sometimes you missed and yer whole head went in and it washed all the black soot off yer face. And ye were half black and half white. And then yer sheep's wool moustache: if it got wet it fell off, and your disguise was nearly gone! Next you had to try and take a bite off a treacle scone hanging on a string. You couldn't use your hands and when you tried to take a bite, this scone started to waggle and it spread all over yer face. By the end of the night we each had a big pillowslip full of nuts and oranges and apples to take home and wir faces all covered with treacle!

To be safe from evil and out of the Devil's reach on Hallowe'en night the Travellers believed you were to *keep within the circle*. If you sat or stood within a circle at Hallowe'en time, before twelve o'clock midnight, suppose it was only a circle of people around a fire, then you were safe from all evil for the incoming year. In the olden days the crofters in the Western Isles used to bring in the ring of a cart wheel, the iron ring, and place it on the floor. All visitors who came to them stood within the wheel on Hallowe'en night. There they probably had a drink and a crack and talk. Because the belief was that within the circle till after twelve o'clock evil couldna cross. It did not matter if the circle was only drawn with your finger on the Earth or drawn above your door or window; but if you werena within that circle on Hallowe'en night then ye had bad luck for the whole year following!

Our greeting today 'hello' comes from 'halloo' or 'hallow'. To me this means 'have you been hallowed -- have you been within the circle for the incoming year?' For Travellers have called Hallowe'en 'The Night of the Circle'.

## Editor's Note

The twenty stories making up this collection of Duncan Williamson's folk tales incorporate the Scottish Travelling People's beliefs about evil, temptation and suffering. Religious expression shines through – these stories are expressive of a traditional attitude towards death. For Duncan, as for all Travellers, life is a simple force, a force deeply felt. It is spurred in the emotive stories Travellers tell and listen to about the Devil – who opposes life and goodness.

Presented in the living language of the storyteller, a vigorous form of traditional storytelling, the folk tale on paper should reveal precisely how a story is nourished. Like the Sun and Earth to an old tree, the storyteller's words and phrases sustain the folk tale. With respect for the antiquity of the tradition, great care has been taken to retain Scottish idioms, syntax, grammar and colloquialisms which feature in the oral stories. All Scottish dialectal and Traveller cant vocabulary is defined in the Glossary.

'Magical incantatory storytelling genius' is the description of Duncan Williamson's narrative used by Scotland's

greatest folklorist of the twentieth century, Hamish
Henderson (see the Introduction to *A Thorn in the King's
Foot*, Penguin, 1987). As custodian of the estate of Duncan
Williamson and editor of his phenomenal repertoire, I hold
his Scottish Traveller storyteller's own, distinctive command
of language in absolute regard. Concerning the demonic
folk tales published in this volume, transcription has been
the Devil's work – recreating the original voice so that words
fly to the ear from a printed page.

Sources of the stories are traditional: they were heard and
learned from members of the storyteller's own extended
family of Travelling People or from close Traveller friends.
Willie Williamson, a cousin of Duncan's father's, told him
'Woodcutter and the Devil', 'Jack and the Devil's Gold', 'The
Challenge' and 'Jack and the Devil's Purse'. These were
heard from old Uncle Willie in Argyll when Duncan was a
boy. The Williamson family then lived in a large handmade
tent or barricade in a forest near Loch Fyne. A river separated their part of the wood from another part where
Travellers like Uncle Willie would come along to camp in
the summer and put up their bow tents. 'We children would
cross the river and go to the Traveller camping places, sit
there and listen,' said Duncan.

Sandy Reid, an uncle on his mother's side, used to camp
in the wood across from the Williamson family in the 1930s.
He told 'The Devil's Coat'. Old Bet MacColl, Duncan's
paternal grandmother, was the source of 'The Tramp and
the Farmer'. 'Jack and the Sea Witch' was among hundreds
of stories told by the famous Traveller storyteller of
Aberdeenshire, the Story-mannie Johnnie MacDonald,
known as 'Old Toots'. He was a cripple and specialised in
storytelling while watching young children for his Traveller
relatives, who would give him accommodation in return for

his help. These stories were first published in *May the Devil Walk Behind Ye!* (Canongate, 1987).

'The Challenge' and 'Jack and the Sea Witch' are among several tales in the collection not specifically about the Devil. But their ethos is quite sinister. Evil manifests itself in a variety of forms in the world. And sometimes the shadow can be quite beautiful to behold, a creature impossible to deny, such as the King of the Mermen, La Mer la Moocht. Another tantalising tale of incredible dimensions is 'Patrick and Bridget', included for its nonsense and delightful play on the headless husband. Tender ghosts from the canine world and eerie characters who have mysterious powers to heal find their place alongside accounts of the Black Art – lethal, true apparitions from the Otherworld.

Throughout the genre of Traveller folk tales there is a distinct lack of moralising. Lessons are intended, but the teaching of a story can be subtle. Awareness of meanings often comes later . . . when you look to yourself!

Finally, a word must be said about the hero of the Traveller tales – Jack. He is the most important character in Duncan Williamson's stories. As Duncan has often explained, 'Jack was not one particular person, but a piece of everyman.' In hundreds of stories about Jack, collected on the storyteller's travels, with one exception the hero is never old. Also with one exception, Jack is never a child; he is almost always either a teenager or a young man. In Traveller tradition Jack never dies; he is always welcome with the king, he is the king's favourite. Sometimes he is lazy or foolish, but often not as foolish as folk think! Built up by the storytellers over countless generations, Jack was a certain kind of person: never afraid, always brave, always handsome and good-looking, even though he lay by the fire and grew a beard and never washed himself. Apart from one story where

Jack's father is an old seaman with a peg-leg, his father is not present. Why does Jack live with his mother? And where does Jack really come from?

The storyteller tells us to look to the stories for the answers. The tales about Jack go back a long, long time. 'Bag of Lies' gives a hint of the source of the Jack tales, but much is left to the imagination of the listener; everything is not laid out like in a children's schoolbook. Like dreams, it's always been a mystery.

Linda Williamson

# The Queen and the Devil

The old queen was very sad, sad at heart because her husband the king had just died. They had reigned together for many years and she'd had a happy life. They only had one son, whom they loved dearly. They were very well thought of, the whole country loved their king and queen and their beautiful young son. The queen appreciated this from her people. She gave great, wonderful parties every now and then to show them that she appreciated their love. But after the king died the queen had become very sad. And her young son the prince saw this, and he got sad too. But he had one obsession: he liked to go hunting.

And one day out on the hunt he fell from his horse. He was hurt severely. The huntsmen carried him back to the palace. They placed him on the bed and there he lay. His back was broken. The old queen was now sadder than ever. Her husband was gone, and now her son, the only being they loved together between them was very seriously ill.

She sat by his bedside and she prayed and she clasped her hands. She prayed to her God and she prayed to everyone. But he got weaker and weaker . . . he finally died.

Now the queen was really very upset. The thought of everything was gone. Never, no more did she show her face before her people in the village. The great palace was there and all the workers in the palace did their things. But the queen just stood by herself. She walked in the garden a sad, lonely old woman. Her husband was bone, her beautiful son was gone. She had no one left in the world. No more did they have parties in the great palace. The great fêtes and the great things were gone. And the people around the country and around the palace got sadder and sadder, because they felt for the queen.

But one day the old queen was walking in the garden admiring her flowers which she'd tended so many times before. The weeds were growing up among them, but now she had no more thought for the flowers in her garden. Then she turned around – there stood behind her this gentleman dressed in black in a long dark cloak.

She said, 'Hello!'

And he said, 'Hello!'

She said, 'Where have you come from?'

'Oh, never mind where I come from, my dear, I've been walking here admiring you. I've been watching you for a few days, and you seem very sad.'

'Oh, I am very sad. Who are you?'

'Oh,' he said, 'I'm just a stranger.'

And she could see that he was dressed in black from head to foot with a long cloak touching the ground. She said, 'Where have you come from?'

'Oh,' he said, 'never mind where I've come from. I have just come to say hello. I can see you're very sad.'

She said, 'Of course there's sadness in my heart, because you know I have lost my husband the king.'

The stranger said, 'I know.' And he smiled to himself.

'And,' she said, 'I've just lost my son!'

'Well . . .' he said.

'He was hurt in a riding accident. I sat beside him, I prayed to my God to help him. But no one could help him. He is gone.'

And the stranger said to her, 'Why are you so sad?'

'Well,' she said, 'why shouldn't I be? My husband is gone and my son is gone. There's nothing left for me in this world.'

'But there are many wonderful things left in the world for you, my dear,' he said. 'You are not really old.'

'But,' she said, 'why should life go on for me? I wish that someone would take me away from this Earth!'

He said, 'Well, maybe that could be arranged.'

She said, 'Who are you?'

'Well, I'm just a stranger. What would you give to be happy again?

She says, 'Happy? I'll never be happy again, never again.'

'Oh yes!' he said. 'Happiness is for everyone.'

'But,' she says, 'how can I be happy? My son is gone and my husband is gone. How . . .'

He said, 'I can make you happy.'

'What are you? Are you a magician or something?'

'No, my dear, I'm not a magician,' he said. 'I'm just a friend, and a stranger.'

'Well, it's nice to be happy, but,' she said, 'where am I going to find happiness?'

'What would you give for happiness?'

She said, 'I'd give anything in this world.'

'Would you give your soul,' he said, 'for happiness?'

'My soul?' she said. 'What is my soul to me, if I have one? I have prayed to my God for my son and He never helped me. If my soul is worth anything I would give it today, if only I could find a little happiness!'

And the stranger said, '*Happiness you shall have*! But I will come and see you again.' And then he was gone.

The queen walked around the garden and she looked all

around. She said, 'These flowers are full of weeds. The gardener has not been tending to the flowers. The trees have never been looked after!'

A great change had come over the queen. She had completely forgotten about everything but her garden. She went out and she told the workers, 'My garden's been neglected. The flowers are covered with weeds and the trees have never been pruned for months. Where are all my workers? What have you done to my garden?'

And when everybody saw that the queen was worried about her garden they rushed to tidy it up. They worked in the garden as hard as they could.

And up goes the queen to her room. She looks all around. She says, 'My room is so untidy!' There were things lying all around the floor. 'Who has done this to my place?' And the queen called for her maids at hand, 'Get my room tidied up at once!'

They tidied up her room. They talked to each other and said, 'What has come over our queen? Something terrible has happened. She is smiling, she is happy once again.'

So the queen walks out to the front of the palace, and it was dreich and barren. Everything looked so dark and grey. She stood over the balcony and she said, 'Where are all my people? Where are all my friends? Why is everyone so sad?'

Everyone looked all around and said, 'A strangeness has come over the queen.'

She said, 'Why is everyone so sad? Where's the party? Where are all my friends? Where are all the guests? Where are all the people?' There was no one. The queen sent word all around the palace: 'Get my people to come before me! Let's have fun. Let's have a party! Let's have a fête! Let's have everything we used to have!'

So word spread around the palace that once again the

queen was happy. And they started, and they set a royal fête where everyone came from all around to see the queen once more. They came from far and wide; they came knights from far off, they came lairds and dukes and people from the village and they were having a great party in front of the palace.

And in amongst them walked the queen, saying hello to everyone and bowing to everyone. Everyone was happy. They had drinking and fêtes and fighting and battles and they had everything – life once again was back to normal. There were jugglers, there were singers, everyone was happy having great fun!

When lo and behold at that very moment, in amongst everyone walked this tall, dark stranger with a long black cloak. And there sat the queen up on her bench before everyone watching everyone enjoying theirself. When he walked up to the queen and said: 'Hello, my dear! Sppst,' he spat and *flame* came from his mouth.

And the queen stood back. She said, 'Who are you?'

He said, 'Who am I? You are bound to recognise me! I have come to see you. You gave me your promise . . . now are you happy?'

'Happy?' she said. 'I'm happier than anyone in the world!'

'Well, I gave you the happiness. Now I have come for you. You must come with me,' and he 'spsst' – spat again and *flames* spat from his mouth.

The queen said, 'Look . . .'

He said, 'Do you remember when I met you in the garden? When you wanted happiness? And you promised me you would give your soul, what I wanted to give you happiness.'

She said, 'Yes.'

'Well, I gave you happiness. Don't you have everything

you had before?' he said. 'And I provided it for you. Now, you must come with me.'

She says, 'No! I can't come with you – I am too happy!'

But he said, 'You promised me!'

She said, 'Guards, arrest this man!' And the guards drew back their bows and arrows to arrest him.

He held out his hand, like *that* – from every finger came the heads of ten snakes with their beady eyes glaring and their fangs and their tongues going out and in, their forked tongues going out and in. And he said: 'Well, let them come to me, my dear!' He held his hand and the tongues of the snakes with the beady eyes . . .

'Use your spears! Use your arrows!' she said.

And they fired! They hit his chest and the spears stotted off like lumps of steel and fell on the ground. And he walked among them with his fingers sticking out – the heads of the snakes. The people cringed in terror back from him. He followed them back, raised his fingers with these ten snakes, their beady eyes and their tongues in front of them.

And the queen sat in terror. Everyone backed away. Then he went up to the queen and he closed his fingers. The snakes were gone.

'Now,' he said, 'my dear, it is time for you to come with me.'

She says, 'No! You are the Devil!'

'Of course,' he said, 'I am the Devil.'

'Well' she said, 'if you're the Devil – I've heard many stories of you. You always give people a chance.'

He said, 'You prayed to your God, didn't you?'

'I prayed to my God to save my son, but He never saved my son.'

'Well,' he said, 'you asked me to make you happy and I

made you happy. Now you have everything you want and you gave me your promise.'

She says, 'Please, if you are the Devil, and the stories I've heard about you . . . please give me one more chance – one more chance I beg of you!'

And the Devil said, 'Of course, I always give people a chance. I'll be back in three weeks' time, my dear. On condition that *you can do something that I can't do,* and failing that, you shall come with me!' And then in a *flash* he was gone.

The queen was upset. She knew she was in touch with the Devil. The Devil had taken over her soul. She told everyone around the palace what was going to happen – the Devil was coming for her in three weeks' time. Could she do something that the Devil could not do?

They came from all parts of the Earth, from all parts of her kingdom telling her this and telling her that, things that she could do to cheat the Devil. The queen listened. But one by one all the things they knew, she knew the Devil could compete against anything she heard. Till she was in tears and worried that the Devil was coming for her.

Then up to her palace came an old shepherd with a little bag on his back and a little bag under his arm and a long grey beard and a ragged coat. He stepped up the stairs. He was stopped immediately by the guards.

And they said, 'Where are you going, old man?'

'Well, I am just an old shepherd and I have come to help the queen.'

So everybody was interested. Anyone who could give help to the queen would be acceptable. So the old shepherd was led up to the queen's chamber. And there sat the queen in great grief, knowing that within a week the Devil was coming to take her.

And the old shepherd stepped up and said, 'Your Majesty,

I am believing you have been in touch with the Devil. And he has challenged you to a great duel, that you could do something that he could not do.'

She said, 'Of course, you have heard, my friend.'

'Well, I am just an old shepherd, my dear, my majesty, and I have come to help you.'

She said, 'No one can help me. I've heard many things from all of my subjects all over the land and nothing that they've said can help me.'

'But,' he said, 'my dear, I can help you.'

And from under his arm he took a very small sheepskin bag, and he held it up to her. He said to her: 'In this little bag, my dear, is something that will help you.'

And the queen took it, the small sheepskin bag. She shaked it. It was full of water. She said to him:

'And what can I do with this, old shepherd?'

He said, 'All you can do with it, my dear, is take it and put it in two halves between two little measures. And wait till the Devil comes back to you again. Ask him to take one drink, and you take the other.'

So the queen thanked the old shepherd and she said, 'If this works, my friend, I will repay you for everything you have done for me. You are only a shepherd, but if this works for me you will never be a shepherd again.'

'Don't worry,' said the old man, 'don't worry about it. Just forget it. But remember what I told you.'

So the old shepherd went on his way. And the queen stood with the little bag. She then kept it within her bedroom, she pressed it to her heart and she blessed it. And soon the time passed. It was time for the Devil to return once again.

She went into the room and she took two little silver glasses, silver drinking glasses, and she halved the water of the little bag in two. She placed them on the table and there she waited. She sat and she waited and soon it was twelve o'clock on the very day that the Devil said he was coming back.

Then there was a *flash* in the room! There he stood once again with his long, dark cloak beside her. He said, 'My dear, I have come back.'

'Oh yes,' she said, 'I know you've come back.'

He said, 'Do you remember what I told you?'

'Yes, I do.'

'Now,' he said, 'you asked for a second chance and I gave it to you. Can you do something I can't do?'

And she said, 'Well, I think I can.'

And she picked up the glasses, the little silver drinking glasses. She passed one to him and she said: 'You drink that one and I'll drink the other.'

The queen lifted it up and she drank it down, and placed the glass on the table. 'Now,' she said, 'Devil, you drink the other half.'

And the Devil put it to his mouth. He tasted it: 'Sppst!' he spat it out.

'Queen, there's no one can make the Devil drink Holy Water!' he said.

And that is the end of my story.

# The Devil's Coat

There was once this old Traveller man and his wife; they travelled, walking mostly round Perthshire. Their two children had grown up and left them and got married. But this old man and his old wife always came back to the same wee place every winter to stay. And they camped in this wee wood by the side of the road. Now, he was a very nice easy-going man and so was the woman. The folk of the district knew them very well and respected them for what they were.

So this year the old man and woman had been away all summer wandering here and there, and the wife had sold stuff from her basket. He'd made baskets and tinware. They'd made their way back once more to their winter camping place. The old wife was hawking the houses with her basket round the doors that she knew and everybody welcomed her, glad to see her back again.

Now this man was an awful nice old man, he was really good. And his old wife really thought the world of him. At the weekend on a Saturday he would walk to the nearby village to the wee bar and have a couple pints of beer. His old wife would sit and do something at home at the camp till he came back. But they'd only been at this place for about a week when it came Saturday, and it landed on Hallowe'en night.

'Maggie,' he said to her, 'I think I'll dander awa along the length o' the town to the pub and hae a couple o' pints, pass the night awa.'

'Well,' she said, 'John, as long as ye dinna be too late. Because I'm kind o' feart when it gets dark at night-time to sit here myself, and especially when it's Hallowe'en. And it bein Hallowe'en night ye ken the Devil's loosed, supposed tae be on Hallowe'en night!'

'You and your Devil,' the old man says, 'ye're awfa superstitious. Ye ken fine there no such a thing as the Devil!'

'Well never mind,' she says, 'I've got my beliefs and you've got yours. But try and get hame as soon as ye can.'

'All right,' says the old man, 'I'll no wait long. I havena much money to spend, a couple o' shillings.' So he says cheerio to his old wife and away he goes.

Now from where they stayed in this wee wood at the roadside he had about a mile to go. But before he came to the wee village there was a burn and a bad bend, and a bridge to cross. So the old man lighted his pipe and walked away to the village and landed at the pub.

He spent his couple o' bob and had a few pints to himself. But he met in with two or three other folk he had known, country folk from about the district that he used to work for and they kept him later than he really thought it was. But it must have been near closing time – he clean forgot about his old wife – it was near about half past ten at night when he finally left the pub. And he wasn't really drunk.

So he dandered home till he came to the bridge, and it was a dark, dark night. Barely a star shining. Just as he came to the bridge before the bad bend he said, 'Everybody says this bridge is haunted, haunted by the Devil. But I dinnae believe in nae devils!'

But just when he came over the bridge and round the bend he seen this thing lying across the middle o' the road in front o' him.

'God bless me,' said the man, 'somebody must be drunk and fell in the road.' But he came up closer to it . . . he seen it was a coat. And the old man picked it up.

'I'll carry it on to the camp,' he said. 'Maybe somebody dropped it, maybe the laird or some o' the gamekeepers goin hame from the pub must hae dropped it. But it's a good coat.' That he could see.

So he travelled on. Home he came. And he had a wee barrikit built up and his wee lamp, the cruisie was going.

The old woman says to him, 'You're kind o' late, where were ye?'

'Ach, Maggie, I met two or three folk in the pub, men I used to work for, do wee bits o' jobs for and they kept me crackin. I'm sorry for bein late.'

'Aye, it's all right yinst you're back. Were ye no feart to come ower that brig?'

'What am I going to be feart of?' he said.

She says, 'Feart o' *Cog, the Devil*! This is Hallowe'en night.'

'Ach, you and your superstition,' he said.

She said, 'What's that you've got there?'

'A coat I found on the brig.'

'Oh,' she said, 'a coat . . . hmm. Let me look at it.' And the old woman looked at it. 'Well, John, I've seen many's a coat, but that's the prettiest coat I've ever seen in my life!'

It was black. It had a black velvet neck, velvet sleeves and velvet pockets. And black shiny buttons, four black shiny buttons.

She said, 'It's a beautiful coat. But I'll tell ye, it must hae fell off some o' the coaches goin to the town. It must be some high-up body's coat that, because that's nae poor man's coat.'

'Well, I've been lookin for a coat like this all my days,' he said.

She says, 'Ye're no goin to keep it are ye?'

'Oh aye, I'm goin to keep it. I'm goin to keep it all right,' he said. 'I've always wanted a coat like this. And naebody'll ever ken I've got it. I'm keepin it!'

'Well,' she says, 'ye might be keeping it, John, but what if somebody comes lookin for it?'

'I'll say I never seen nae coat on the road,' he said. 'I want it and I'm goin to keep it!'

'Oh well,' she says, 'please yersel!'

So the old man had his tea. He sat cracking to his old wife a wee while and sat telling her about the folk he met in the pub and that. He went to bed. It was a cold night, a cold frosty night.

'Maggie,' he said, 'I'm goin to fling that coat ower the top of the bed to keep us warm.'

'Ah well,' she says, 'it'll ay help, it's a cold night.'

So after the old man and the old woman had made their bed the old man flung the coat over the top of them. But he was lying smoking for a wee while his pipe and the old man rose to go outside. He was a good wee while out, and all in a minute he heard a scream. He ran back. And there was the old woman, she's sitting and shaking with fright!

'God bless us, woman,' he said, 'what's wrong wi ye?'

'Dinna speak to me . . . it's that coat!' she said.

'Aye, coat! There nothing wrong wi the coat!'

'No,' she said, 'maybe you dinna ken there nothin wrong with it – these four buttons that's on that coat – when you were out they turned into four eyes and they were shinin at me and winkin at me!'

'Ah, ye must hae fell asleep while I was outside doin a wee job to myself,' he said.

'No, Johnnie, no, I never fell asleep. I'm tellin you, that coat's haunted – that's *the Devil's coat* frae the haunted brig!'

'Na, woman, you ought to have more sense than that.'

But the old man lay down again. He happed the coat back over him. But during the night he turned to the old woman:

'Maggie, do you no feel it's awfa warm?'

'Aye,' she said, 'it's awfa warm.'

'God bless us,' he said, 'the sweat's breakin off me and it's a cold night like this!'

'I tellt ye,' she said, 'it's that *coat*.'

'Aye, the coat! Lie down and hap yourself and pull the coat up!'

But the old man tossed and turned and he moaned all night. And he wakened up. The sweat was lashing off him and so was his old woman.

'Maggie,' he said, 'it's an awfa warm night!'

She said, 'It's no warm – it's a frosty winter's night!'

'Well,' he said, 'lie back down.'

Now the old man began to get kind o' umperant and cheeky to the old woman. Every word the woman said he began to lose his temper. Now he never was like this to the old woman before. But during the night he said, 'Woman, would ye get off the top o' me?'

She says, 'I'm no near ye.'

He said, 'You were lying on top o' me a minute ago. I felt the weight o' you on top o' me!'

She says, 'No!' And the old woman rose up. She was wet with sweat and so was he. She said, 'It's that *coat*!'

'God curse you and the coat,' he said.

And he catcht the coat and flung it at the foot o' the bed. And it lay down at the foot o' the bed. The old man fell asleep and so did his old wife. And he wakened up. He was frozen, cold as could be.

'God bless us,' he said, 'it's awfa cold. I'm frozen.'

She said, 'You were sweatin a minute ago an' complainin about somebody lyin a-top o' you.

And he started to the old woman, gave the woman the most cheek and umperance in the world. And he was going to hit her. 'Only for you,' he said, 'I could hae my coat ower the top o' me! You and this silly mental carry on o' ye – you and your mad beliefs!'

'Well, you'll no believe me – it's that *coat*! The best thing ye can do is get rid o' it, or I'm no goin to bide in the camp wi ye wi it nae mair.'

'I'm keeping the coat and you shut up!' He'd never said that to his old wife before in his life.

But the next morning the old woman got up, kindled the fire and made a wee cup o' tea. She offered the old man a cup o' tea.

'Leave it down there. I'll get it when I'm ready,' he said.

The woman looked at him. He never was like that with her before. But the more the week passed . . . the old woman went away and done a bit hawking, came back. But no: the fire was out, the old man was sitting at the fire. He'd hardly speak to her and snapped at every word she said to him.

'John,' she said, 'what's comin over you?'

He said, 'There nothing coming over me, nothing at all.'

She said, 'Ye're demented some way.'

He said, 'I'm no demented.'

She said, 'Did ye look . . . were there anything in the pockets o' that coat you found in the road?'

'Aye, there were something in one pocket. But you're no gettin it. I'm keepin it!'

She says, 'What was it?'

He says, 'A sixpence, a silver sixpence, and I'm keepin it, you're no gettin it. Dinna ask it!'

He said, 'Ah well,' says the old woman, 'I canna dae nothin with you. The best thing ye can dae is go back and put that coat where you got it.'

'No,' he says, 'I'm no puttin the coat where I got it. I'm goin to keep it, suppose it is the Devil's coat, I'm keepin it!'

'Oh well,' she said, 'it's up to yourself.'

But the days passed by and the old man got worse every day. He got so that the old woman couldn't put up with him. Her life was greetin terrible with him for nearly a week. The old man was demented and the old woman couldn't get a minute's peace with him. Every night . . . the coat over him, the coat off him, the coat over him, the coat off him. And the old woman wouldna bide in the tent with the coat for God!

But one day she says to herself, 'I canna take this nae longer. Either he goes or I go. If the coat disna go, I'll go!' she tellt the old man.

'You can go if you want,' he said, 'but I'm keepin the coat.'

'Oh well . . .' she said.

The woman lifted her wee basket and away she went. She wandered away down to an old woman she knew, an old henwife who kept hens on a wee croft.

Out comes the woman: 'Oh it's yourself, Maggie,' she says.

'Aye.'

'Ye back for the winter?'

'Aye, I'm back for the winter.'

'Well, ye're just in time. I was cleaning up and haein a wee cup o' tea. Come on in and hae a wee cup o' tea wi me,' she said. So this old hen woman liked old Maggie awful much. She said, 'I'll hae a look for some stuff to ye afterward.' The old woman made her a cup o' tea and gave her scones and cheese.

'Oh, by the way, how is old John getting on?' she says. 'Is he keepin all right?'

'No,' says Maggie, 'he's no keepin all right, to tell ye the truth. There's something far wrong with him.'

Oh, God bless me,' says the old henwife, 'he's no ill is he?'

No,' says the old woman, 'he's no ill. No ill nae way ... he's worse than ill – he's demented. And bad and wicked.'

'Well,' says the old henwife, 'it's a droll thing. I've kent old John for many's a year. He used to come here and dig my garden and cut sticks for me, do a wee bit job for me. And there's no a nicer old man that ever walked the country. Everybody in the district has got a great name about him.'

'Well,' Maggie says, 'he's a changed man today. Ever since he found that *coat*.'

'What coat?' says the old henwife.

So the old woman up and tellt her the story.

'Oh,' she said, 'did he look the pockets out?'

'Aye, he looked the pockets out.'

She said, 'What was in the pocket o' the coat?'

'A sixpence.'

'Ah,' the old henwife said, 'a sixpence, aye ... What kind o' coat was it?'

She tellt her: 'Long and black, velvet neck, velvet pockets and four black-horned shiny buttons. And to mak it worse, the night he brung it back old John went outside for a wee walk to hisself, an' I looked. As low as my mother,' she says to the old woman, 'I'll no tell you a lie, but I could swear on the Bible these four buttons turned into four eyes and they were winkin and blazin at me!'

'God bless me,' says the old henwife, 'where did he get it?'

Maggie says, 'He found it on the bridge, the haunted bridge goin to the village.'

'Oh aye,' said the old woman, 'hmmm. Well, I'll tell ye, the morn's Sunday and I'm goin to the church to the village.

Would it be all right if I take a wee walk in and see you on the road past?'

'I wish to God you would, and try and talk some sense into him,' she says.

'I'll drop in and hae a wee crack to old John on the road past when I'm goin to the church.'

'All right,' says Maggie.

So the henwife gave the old Traveller woman eggs and butter and a can o' milk and everything she needed. She bade her farewell and away went Maggie home to the camp.

When she came home the old man's sitting cross-legged with the coat beside him. He wouldn't hardly speak to her. No fire, his face no washed or nothing. And his two eyes were rolling in his head. The old woman kindled the fire and made him some tea. She offered . . .

'No,' he said, 'I'm no wantin nothing fae ye. Don't want nothing fae ye, not nothing at all!'

'God bless me, John,' she said, 'that's no a way to carry on. What's wrong wi ye?'

'There's nothing wrong wi me. What's wrong with *you*?'

'Oh,' she said, 'there nothing wrong with *me*.'

But anyway, that night again the old woman wouldn't let him put the coat over the bed. And they argued all night about it. The old man gave in at last. He flung it at the foot o' the bed.

But next morning the old woman got up again, made a cup o' tea. The old man took a cup o' tea, nothing else, hardly speaking, just snapping at every word she spoke to him.

'Well, John,' she said, 'there's something far wrong with you, since ever you found that coat. As low as my father, that is *the Devil's coat*!'

'I'm no carin,' he said, 's'pose it's *the Devil's father's coat*. I'm keepin it!'

'Well,' she said, 'if you keep it, you canna keep me.'

'Well,' he said, 'if it comes to the choice, you ken where your family is. You can go and stay with them – I'll stay wi my coat.'

The old woman couldn't see what to do with him. But they were still arguing away when up comes the old henwife with her wee hat and coat on and her handbag in one hand, her prayer book and Bible in below her oxter. It was only two steps off the road to the wood where the old man and woman were staying. The old henwife stepped in.

She said, 'Hello, Maggie, how are ye?'

'Oh,' she said, 'hello!'

She spoke to old John, 'Hello, John, how are ye?'

'Oh, I'm no so bad, I'm no any better wi you askin anyway! Ye'll be up here for me to do some mair cheap work for ye – work for you for nothin.'

'No, John,' she says, 'I'm no up tae gie ye mair work for nothing.' The old woman was dubious right away. The old man was never like this before. 'To tell ye the truth, John, I'm a bit worried. Maggie was down crackin to me yesterday and she tellt me about the coat you found at the bridge.

He said, 'She had nae right tellin ye about the coat. I warned her not to tell naebody about it.'

'Well, John,' she said, 'I want to see it.

He said, 'Do you want to . . . do ye ken somebody belongin to it?'

'No,' she said, 'I dinna ken naebody belongin to it. But I want to see it.'

So the old man went out and he got the coat. He held it up.

The old henwife came up close to him: she said, 'Hold that up by the neck!'

He held it up. She looked it up and down. She looked at it

a long, long while. She could fair see it was just sleek and shining like sealskin.

She says, 'John, what did you do with the sixpence you got in the pocket o' it?'

'Oh,' he says, 'did that old bitch o' mine tell ye that too? Well, I've got it in my pocket and I'm keepin it.'

She says, 'John, I want ye to do something for me.'

He says, 'What is it?'

She says, 'I want you to put that sixpence back in the pocket and hold up the coat!'

The old man looked at her for a long while. But something came over him when he looked at her . . . the way the old henwife looked at him. And he got kind o' calm and quiet. He held up the coat by the neck. He dropped the sixpence in the coat pocket. The old man opened the other pocket and the old woman dropped in the Bible.

Well, when she dropped the Bible into that coat pocket the coat jumped about ten feet in the air! And the arms started to flap, and it was up and down and running about same as it was demented. Till the old woman said to old John:

'Run and catch it! Stand on it!'

The old man got a terrible fright and old Maggie got a terrible fright. The old man was shaking like the leaf o' a tree and so was the old woman. The old man began to realise now there was something far wrong with this coat.

So the old man stood on it with his feet. And the old woman leaned down. She put her hand in the pocket and took the Bible out.

'Now, John,' she said, 'I'll tell ye; I'm goin to the church. You walk along with me to the bridge. Take that coat wi ye.'

Old Maggie said, 'I'm no bidin here myself. I'll walk wi yese.' So, the three o' them walked along to the bridge.

And the old woman said: 'Where did ye find the coat?'

He says, 'I found it just there – that bad bend, the dark corner at the bridge. It was lyin across the road.'

So the old woman says, 'Roll it up in a knot!'

And the old man rolled it up like that.

'Now,' she says, 'throw it over the bridge!' And the old woman opened the Bible and she said:

'*God bless us all*!' while the old man flung the coat over the bridge. When it hit the water it went in *a blaze o' fire* and disappeared.

The old man looked: 'God bless me,' he said to the old woman, 'it definitely was *the Devil's coat*.'

So the old henwife said, 'Aye John, that was *the Devil's coat*. That was lost when he came here on Hallowe'en night. But it never was lost. It was left 'specially for you: if you'd hae spent that sixpence, you'd hae been with the Devil!'

'Well,' he said to the old woman, 'thank God you saved me.'

And the old man put his arm round his old wife and the two o' them walked home. The old man said to her, 'Look, as long as I live, Maggie, never again will I cross that brig at night-time.'

And from that day on the old man never crossed that bridge again till whatever day he died. He was the nicest old man to his old wife in the world. And life went on as if nothing ever had happened.

And that's the last o' my wee story.

# Boy and the Knight

In the West Coast of Scotland is Loch Awe. And in that loch is a castle, ruins now – just ruins – the walls are there but nothing else. The castle is called 'Woe be tae ye', what I was told, and no one as far as I know has ever known where it really began. But during the rainy season in Argyll the castle is surrounded by water, but when it comes a dry summer the loch dries up and ye can walk to the castle across the beach – which is only a fresh-water loch – it sits on about half an acre of land. And there's such beautiful grass round the island.

So, a long time ago there lived an old widow and her son, they had a little croft on the mainland on Loch Aweside. She'd only one son, her husband had died many years ago and left her the one son. But she had some goats and some sheep and some cattle, and they had a wonderful life together. But her son was just about ten years old, and he had so many goats they had no food for them.

So one day she said, 'Son, take the goats out to find some food for them.'

'Mummy,' he says, 'why don't I take them down to the island?'

She said, 'Son, you can't get tae the island today; the water is not low enough tae get across to the island.'

He says, 'Mummy, I think after a dry spell, I think we could get across.'

So the young boy takes about five or six goats and they all follow him because they knew him as a baby. And the water then was only about two inches deep because it had been a dry summer. He walks across onto the little island in the middle of Loch Awe. The castle is surrounded by all these beautiful grasses and daisies and things, he thought it would be a wonderful place to take his goats and give them a good feed. And his mother had decided that he could go.

So wonst he led the goats across they spread out and they were eating, eating as fast as possible this beautiful green grass, because on their little croft they had eaten all the grass down. So the young boy walks round the castle, he's looking up at the walls and he's wondering in his own mind what kind of people had lived in this a long time ago, long before his time? And he walks round the walls, there were stairs going up, the stairs were half broken, there was no roof on the castle and some stairs had fallen in, there were big boulders and rocks. And then there was a small chamber that led into another room.

While his goats were busy feeding he would walk around, and he walked in through this passage to a chamber of the castle – even though the roof was gone there was a big broad square – which might in the olden days have been a dining room for the castle. And lo and behold he walked in . . .

There lying on the floor was a suit of armour!

And the boy wondered, he says, 'I've never been here before, but – a suit of armour lying on the floor of the castle? I must tell my mummy about this when I go back.' It was only a common suit of armour as far as he was concerned.

*He was a knight, and round his waist was a belt and in the belt was a sword.*

The boy walked all around the place . . . so far as he was concerned, it was just a suit of armour. And he looked, he saw the sword and he thought tae himself . . . his mother had told him many wonderful stories about knights that he heard all the time . . . an' he thought, how in the world could anybody handle a sword like that?

So he walked over, naturally, and he pulled the sword a wee bit out of the sheath by the knight's side, and he pulled it about five inches – then the head of the knight came up! And the boy stopped, he stood there, boy never gave it a thought. He pulled the sword up another bit, to see how long the sword was – and lo and behold the knight sat up like *this* – his legs are stretched out and he sat up, he held straight up!

And he spoke to the boy, he said, 'Pull it out!'

The boy stood back.

The sword was half-drawn from the sheath at his side, he says, 'Pull it out, boy; pull it out, boy!'

And the boy stood there, he was amazed!

He said, 'Pull the sword, boy! Pull it out!'

Boy said . . . he was terrified – he wouldn't pull it out.

'Pull it out,' the knight said, 'an' I'll make ye the riches' man in the worl'!'

The boy wis terrified, ye see – cuidna pull it or go back doon!

'A'll give ye everything you require,' said the knight, an' he wis sittin on his end. 'I'll give ye everything ye want!'

And the boy was so afraid that the knight was going to do him harm, he took the sword and he pushed it back, pushed it back into the sheath, like *that*.

And like that the knight fell back – like *that*.

And the boy looked around . . . there was nothing. Gone was the knight and gone was everything. And the boy was so terrified, he collected his goats and hurried back to his mother on Loch Aweside!

He told his mother the same story as I'm telling you. And his mother turned round. She said, 'Look—'

'Mother,' he said, 'what would hev happened if I'd hae pulled the sword out?'

She says, 'Son, I'm glad you put the sword back, because it's a long, long legend I will want to tell you. Because a long time ago, as far as my great-grandfather an' my grandfather tellt me, there lived a knight in that castle across there, and he stole away a young woman tae be his bride, he took her to that castle. An' he hung his sword on the wall, an' her brothers came to take her back. They surrounded him an' killed him – they never gave him a chance to get his hand on his sword. They killed him because he couldna reach his sword. But if he'd hae reached his sword he could have defended hissel. Son,' she said, 'if you'd hae pulled that sword out, you'd prob'ly done something an' let his soul go in peace. But son, please for my sake, never go back to that castle again!'

And neither the boy ever did. And that castle is called 'Woe be tae ye'. It means *no one enter* – in Gaelic.

And that is a true story.

# The Challenge

Now my story takes you back a long time ago to a village in the north of Scotland. It was served by the local community, all farming folk, who came from outlying regions and hill farms. And in this small village there was only one inn where the farmers and shepherds and ploughmen came for a drink on a Saturday evening. At the end of the village was the churchyard that served the whole community. Not only were the people who died in the village buried in the church-yard, but also the farmers of the outlying regions were buried in this cemetery.

So they gathered one evening in the inn. Farmers, shep-herds, hill workers, peat cutters came in for their usual weekend at the pub. And they stood there and they had their drinks, they had their talks and they discussed many wonderful things. One by one they all finally moved away to go back to their homes.

But there were about a dozen of them left. And the subject they were discussing was the graveyard outside the village, how many people were buried in the cemetery, how long had the people been buried in it, how old it really was.

And then someone spoke up and said, 'How about the ghost?'

And they said, 'The ghost!'

Oh, everyone knew of the ghost. Many people in the village had reported seeing a ghost at the gate of the grave-yard many nights. Many people had seen it, but nobody would believe them.

But in the bar was a girl named Margaret. Now, Margaret was a shepherdess who worked for a local farmer. And she was as good as any man – she could clip a sheep as quick as any man, cowp a sheep on its back and clip it, she could cut peats, she could do anything. She was neither feart o' God, man or the Devil! And they respected her. She was just a young unmarried woman. She was as strong as any man. And she was one of the last ones left in the pub discussing with the men about the local cemetery.

So the subject got around about the ghost. And it was the owner of the inn who spoke up:

'I bet ye there's not one among yese would even go to the graveyard at twelve o'clock! Yese are all standing there talking about it. But there not one among yese who would go up to the graveyard and even view the ghost close up!'

Then up spoke Maggie: 'Look, mister,' she said to the pub owner, 'I'm not feart o' neither ghost, man or the Devil. And I'll go to the graveyard, and if there is a ghost there I'll wait. And if it comes I'll tell ye what I'll do wi ye: I'll bring ye back his shroud or his cloth that he keeps himself white with – we all ken a spirit or a ghost needs something to cover him to keep white – it's no his skeleton folk sees! I'll go up and I'll bring it back to ye. I'll put it on the bar, then will you believe it?'

'No,' he says, 'no, Maggie, no way. Please don't do it! We're only makin fun.'

She says, 'Look, yese are all supposed to be brave men. Ye're all supposed to be great heroes, among the whole crowd o' yese while yese hae got a drink in yese. But I'm no a man, but I'm no feart o' God, man or the Devil. And I'll go tonight providin you keep the pub open till after twelve o'clock. And if there's a ghost there, if he's standing at the gate and if he has a shroud or a sheet on him – I'll bring it back to ye – and fling it ower yer bar!'

'Well,' he said, 'Maggie, if that's the way ye want it. I'll tell ye, I'll mak it better for ye: I'll mak a wager wi ye. If there's such a thing as men hae been reportin about, and if you see a ghost and you bring it back – his shroud to me and put it on the bar – I'll mak it worth your while. I'll give ye five guineas and a bottle o' whisky to yersel!'

She says, 'Done!'

So they sat there and they drank and the clock on the wall said a quarter to twelve. Now in these bygone times the inn owners could keep their pubs open the whole night through, as long as there were people standing to drink.

So she said goodbye to them at the bar and she walked up to the graveyard gate. She stood. She heard the clock in the village striking twelve o'clock as she stood at the gate.

And then across from the gate she saw something white standing with a long shroud on it. And being Maggie, who was neither feart o' God, man, beast or the Devil, she walked up and said, 'Ye're the ghost that's frightening everybody, aren't ye? Well, ye canna frighten me!'

And she catcht the cloot that was ower him, a white shroud, and she pulled it off him. And she put it under her oxter.

There he stood in front o' her, a naked skeleton, nothing but the bones.

And she turned her back on him, she walked onwards. As she's walking on he's coming behind her step after step saying, *'Thoir dhomh air ais mo léine – give me my sheet, I'm cold!* She said, 'Ye'll get nae sheet from me.' And on she walked.

And he walked on after her. 'Oh, give me my sheet,' he was crying. '*Thoir dhomh air ais mo léine – give me my sheet, I'm cold, I'm cold, give me back my sheet.*'

So they walked on till they came to the inn. And the door of the inn was open. He was coming closer and closer to her . . . by this time she began to get kind o' feart that there was really something behind her terrible. And she couldna stand his voice any longer.

He was saying, '*Thoir dhomh air ais mo léine – give me my sheet, I'm cold*!

And she could see the lights. Now by this time she was feart! Really feart, terrified. But she still kept the sheet under her oxter. And she came up to the door of the inn. And she couldna stand it any longer:

'Well,' she says, 'ye've followed me far enough – there's yer sheet!'

Now, he had no power to touch her till he got his sheet back. But as quick as you could draw a breath he picked up that sheet, wrapped it round him and as she was disappearing inside the door of the inn – and the last part of her was her foot going in through the door – he came down on her foot with his hand! He cut her heel, the last part to disappear into the light, and cut the heel off her.

She staggered into the inn and collapsed before all the people in the inn. And they rushed round her. There was her heel cut completely off as if it had been done with a knife. This woman was Maggie, she was a herdswoman, a powerful woman, who was as powerful as any man. She sat there in silent agony with her heel gone.

So they asked her what happened, and she told them the story. She'd pulled the sheet from the wreft, or the skeleton. And she told them it had followed her to the inn. She couldna withstand it any longer, she had to throw him the sheet.

And they said, 'Why didn't you bring the sheet in, and he would never hae touched ye.'

But that was her mistake. Anyhow, she got her five guineas and the bottle of whisky. A cart and horse came to take her back to the farm where she lived.

But after that, that great Maggie, the woman who was as powerful as any man, who could clip sheep, dig drains, do anything, who was neither feart o' God or man or the Devil, just sat there in her chair, a cripple for three months. Never able to do another thing.

And then three months later she was found hanged by the neck in the farmer's barn. She hanged herself on a rope. And the story went on . . .

When people reported later, when they came to the pub, let it be true or a lie, that sometimes when they were passing by the gate of the graveyard coming home, let them be drunk or sober, they saw the reflection of not one white thing standing at the gate of the graveyard, but *two*.

# Wee Black Hen

A long time ago, long before your time and mine, there wonst lived a rich farmer. This farmer was very well off. He had worked hard all his life and had everything his heart desired. But he had also three grown-up sons. There was Willie and Sandy and the youngest laddie, Jack. Now, the three sons had worked for their father all their lives. Even Jack. Jack wasn't lazy; Jack was very clever. In fact, the father had great respect for them all. But because there were three sons, one night he and his wife were sitting talking things over.

'Look, I'm getting too old for running this place,' he said. 'Me and you could get a wee house in the village. We could give the farm to the laddies. They could run it for themselves.'

And the mother says, 'Aye, that'll be fine, husband. But what about the fighting, the squabbling and arguing that'll go on between them if you give it to the three of them?'

'Well, I can't give it to one of them and leave the other two with nothing.' So he thought it over for a wee while and he said, 'I've got a better idea. The three of them are single. None of them's got a wife. And none of them's courting any lassies in the village that I ken about. So I'll tell you what I'll do, wife. I'll call them before me in the morning and I'll make it plain. I'm going to send them into the world, each in a different direction. And I want them to go and seek their own fortunes for one year. I'm sending them out to seek wives for themselves. And the one that brings the most handsome young woman back for their wife will get the farm! And then there'll be no squabbling.'

Oh, the old woman was overjoyed. She thought this was a wonderful idea. So they went to their bed. The old man and woman chatted away all night and thought it was a good idea.

She was ay thinking, 'What about Jack? Jack's kind o' bashful and he's kind o' young.' Jack would be about eighteen at the time.

'Ah well,' he said, 'Jack'll just have to take his chance along with the rest.'

So the next morning when the old woman got up she put breakfast, ham and eggs and stuff down for the laddies. They were all sitting round the old wooden table in the kitchen. And after the farmer had finished his breakfast and leaned back: 'Laddies,' he said, 'I want to tell you something this morning.'

So the laddies were waiting to get their jobs, what their father wanted done.

He said: 'Me and your mother's been thinking. I'm getting kind o' old for this farm and we want to take a wee cottage in the village. And we want to leave the farm to youse. But we can't leave it to the three o' youse. Because I ken what like it will be; there'll be two or more arguing. You'll be wanting to do this and you'll be wanting to do that. And things will never work out. So me and your mother have thought o' a plan. We're going to give you each a bit o' money to keep you going, and send you each out into the world. Now I want youse each to go in a different direction. One go east, one go west, one go north

or south, I don't care. But youse are no' all going the same
way. And to make sure, I'm going to send youse out a day
after each other, ahind each other. Now the one who brings
back the most beautiful young woman to be their wife in
the one year to the day that you leave this house, the one
that brings back the bonniest and handsomest young
woman to this house before me and your mother will get
the whole farm to themselves for the rest of their life! And
I'll pay for all the arrangements for a good wedding day.
I'll give you all everything you require. We'll have a great
session, a great get-together when youse all return. But
youse must all return a year from the day, because I must
have only one wedding day. So will you do that for me? Do
youse agree to that?'

'Oh, Father!' they said, and they thought it was a wonderful
idea.

'Now all come on,' he says, 'before me and your mother,
shake hands on it!'

So the three laddies shook hands across the table. The
agreement was made.

'Now,' he says 'remember, if one o' youse comes back with
a bonnie wife and the other two come back with nothing,
there'll be no squabbling!'

They made their promise to their father.

So that day the old farmer went up and got a puckle
money. And it was Sandy, the oldest brother.

'Right, Sandy,' he says, 'there's your money. Take as many
clothes with you as you want. Now off you go! I'll send
Willie off the morn. What direction are you going, son?'

'Ach, Father,' he says, 'I'll go north.'

So they bade him goodbye at the door and away he went.

The next day it was Willie's turn. So Willie stood at the
door. The old farmer gave him money. And he took a wee

puckle clothes with him, whatever he wanted, a few things he got from his mother to keep him along the road.

'What way are you going now, Willie?' the old farmer says.

'Ach,' Willie says, 'I'll go east.'

'All right,' the farmer says, 'mind you go! Remember, a year and a day you'd better be back here, wife or no wife!'

So off Willie went.

Now the third day it was Jack's turn. The old man and woman came to the door. You ken, the old woman was near in tears because this was her youngest laddie!

'God knows what'll happen to them,' she says. 'They could get into trouble and they could spend all their money . . . God knows what'll happen to them!'

But the old farmer says, 'We made the plan, didn't we? Well, you agreed with it as much as I did.'

So he gave Jack his money. Jack kissed his mother, shook hands with his father.

'Where are you going, brother?' he says to Jack.

'Ach, Father, I'll go west. I'll follow the wind.'

So anyway, we'll have to start with Sandy, the eldest brother. Sandy travels on and on he goes. A couple of days going here and going there. And Sandy was a good worker. He came to this farm and he asked for lodgings.

'Oh,' the farmer said, 'I'll give you lodgings, laddie.'

He had travelled for two days. He was well away from where his father and mother were. 'I'll give you lodgings, fine. But you'll have to do me a wee bit work first.'

'Oh,' Sandy said, 'I'm willing to work!'

'You'd better come in,' he said, 'and have something to eat then.'

So he brought him in to the table. And the first thing

turned in was this young woman, a bonnie-looking young lassie. And she's serving. She's looking at Sandy and putting all these tasty things in front o' him. Sandy looked and eyed her up and down.

'Aye,' he says, 'she's no bad. She's no bad at all! That would suit me fine!' So he sat and cracked to the old farmer. He told him, 'I'll do all the work you want. In fact, I'm looking for a job.' The farmer was so pleased with Sandy's work, within a week Sandy stayed there. He bade with the old farmer.

So Willie travelled away, on and on. He travelled on and the next day he came to a big town. But what happened? With the walking didn't the sole fall off his boot! So in bygone days in the wee streets in the villages there were always cobblers. They called them the 'souter', for mending folk's boots. And this was the first sign he saw above a door. The sole was dragging on his boot.

He said, 'I'll have to get this fixed. I can't go farther without getting this boot fixed.' So Willie goes into the cobbler's shop. There's an old man with a leather apron on, and he's chapping away at the back o' the counter. Willie waited.

But the old man was taking too long. And Willie was giving a big cough to let the old man know he was there. The old man looked round, an old man with grey hair down his back.

'What can I do for you, laddie?' said this old man.

'Well, to tell you the truth, I've been travelling a long, long way, old fellow, and the sole fell off my boot. I wonder, could you fix it for me?'

'Aye, laddie, nae bother. I've an awful lot of work on. But seeing you're here to wait for it, I'll do it for you. Sit down on the chair!'

There was a big, old-fashioned wooden chair. Willie sat

down. And he took off his boot, gave it to the old cobbler. The cobbler put it on the three-legged man, the last, and he ran his hand around the sole. But just then Willie saw the curtain parting – at the back of the shop there was no door, just a curtain. And out comes this bonnie lassie with a tray with two mugs on it. Willie looked at her. Bonniest lassie he's ever seen in his life! The old cobbler's daughter.

So the old cobbler says to his lassie, 'Bring another cup. We've got a young man here. It'll be a wee while before his boot's ready. Get another mug for him!'

The lassie went, parted the curtain and came back with another mug of tea. They sat and they cracked and they cracked. Willie tellt the cobbler his father was a farmer, and he tellt him the whole story.

'Well,' the cobbler said, 'what kind o' work are you used to doing?'

'Well,' said Willie, 'I help my father. My job was mostly sorting the harness on the farm, mending the saddles and the bridles. On a rainy day.'

'Ah,' said the old cobbler, 'if you ken about leather, laddie, you're just the very man I want. Look beside me there! I've got so much work on boots, so much leather to cut, I can't do it all myself. You wouldn't be looking for a job, would you?'

'Oh, I could do with a bit job,' Willie says. 'I'm running kind o' short of money.'

And the old man says, 'Look, there's an empty room upstairs. You can eat with me and my daughter. She lost her mother when she was a wee wean, and I brought her up myself.'

Willie's heart began to beat quick. He swallowed his spittle. He could hardly crack to the old man she was that bonnie, this lassie!

'All right,' he said, 'old fellow, that would suit me fine.'

'You got any bundles or baggage?' said the old man.

Willie said, 'Just two or three sarks.'

'Give them to the lassie there. She'll take them, give them a bit wash to you seeing you've been on the road for a while. And come on upstairs!'

There was a wee wooden stair at the side of the shop. And there was a beautiful wee room at the top with a bed in it, and a wash hand basin. Willie said to himself, 'This is fine for me. I'm going no farther. I've found what I want.'

So we'll leave Willie for a wee while.

Now Jack, after he had bade goodbye to his father and mother, took the puckle money in his pocket. Happy-go-lucky, he wasn't worrying a damn what he did.

He said, 'A year's a long time. I can enjoy myself in a year!'

So Jack travelled on and travelled on, having a bit drink here in the pub and a bit carry-on here and there. And och, three months passed by, just passed like that! Another three months passed and he got two-three jobs, and he wouldn't settle in a job. But he travelled on till he had no more money left, not a penny. He was broke.

And he's coming up this road, oh, many many miles away from where he had left his father and mother. This road goes up by this big estate and there's two big gates.

'There must be a farm up here o' some kind,' he said. 'Maybe two or three farms. I'm needing to look for a job. I'll have to get a job o' some kind to get something to eat.'

He was starving. He had spent all his money. But the first thing he passed was a great big mansion house. Curtains all drawn. There was not a soul about. The grass was growing round about it. It looked derelict.

Jack said, 'Nobody lives in there. It was used at one time. Whoever owns it made it a good house.'

He looked all around. There were turrets on it, oh, great fancy windows and everything. The gates were closed.

'Tsst,' Jack said, 'it's a pity a good house like that is going to waste. I wonder why somebody doesn't bide there?'

But he passed by the house and he hadn't gone far around a bend till he came to a bonnie wee farm at the corner where he took the bad bend. A bonnie wee farm and a wee road running up to it. And all these hens running about. And cockerels. The reek coming from the lum. It all looked so homely and so clean.

Jack said, 'I wonder who lives up here? Some old gadgie and old mort. Maybe I'll get a wee bit day's work or a puckle something to eat from them anyway.'

So he went up to the door and the first thing came out was an old fat woman with a sheet apron round her waist and her cheeks full of flour. She was baking.

She said, 'Well, what can I do for you, laddie?'

He tellt the story to her. He said, 'Look, missus, I'm hungry and I'm looking for a wee bit job.'

'Oh well,' she says, 'I'll tell you the truth, I could do with somebody! Look, my old man fell and broke his leg. I tellt the old dottering soul many times . . .'

She was the cheeriest old woman Jack had ever met! She reminded Jack a wee bit of his mother. She said, 'Would you like to come in and I'll give you something to eat, laddie? I'm just making some scones.'

So she brought Jack into the wee kitchen of the farm house. And there sitting in the chair was the cheeriest old man, a wee fat, round-faced man with rosy cheeks. And he had his leg sticking out wrapped in bandages. His leg was up on the top of a stool.

She says to her man, 'John, a young laddie at the door – he's hungry. He's come a long way. He's looking for a wee bite to eat and he's looking for any kind of job.'

'Job?' he says, 'Oh, God bless us! I wish I was able.'

'I tellt you,' she said, 'you dottering old fool, if you hadn't been rushing about so much – I tellt you one of these days you would fall and break that leg of yours!'

'Sit down, laddie!' the old man says. And the old man took out his pipe and lighted it, a clay pipe. 'Where do you come from?'

So Jack tellt him the whole story and about his two brothers.

'Ah well, laddie,' he says 'there's no women here except my old wife. I don't think your father'd be awful pleased with her!' He said, 'Look, I could do with you. I could really do with you. And I'll pay you well. You'll get plenty to eat here and we've all we need, but I need somebody to help my old wife round the farm. There's cows to milk, byres to clean, hay to cut and things to do. I'll never get it done in the world! But I'm sorry there's no women about the village, the town, o' no kind. Maybe you could get into the big town about nine miles away. You might meet a lassie to please you. I don't want you to get a lassie in the first place . . . I could do with you here!'

'Ach,' says Jack, 'it'll no matter. I'll stick it for a day or two anyway. See what happens.'

But for the first week Jack worked away. And the old man was delighted and the old woman laid praises upon him to the old man. He was so good that laddie, oh, he was just like a son to her. He helped her with the milk and carried basins to her, carried pails for her. He was so good. But the thing was, they had no place for Jack to stay.

The old farmer said, 'Look, you see that big house you passed by?' It was only about twenty yards down the road from the corner where the bad bend was. He said, 'That house belonged to my uncle. I don't remember him, not very much about him. Because you see he was always overseas. He and his daughter used to go off on holidays. But they never came back. He always went on holidays into the East. And the house is probably as much mine as it is theirs now. But I've got the key. And there's plenty bedrooms in it. It's fully fitted. And look, Jack, you can stay down there. There's a good fireplace. Plenty firewood. You can have it to yourself to stay in as long as you want.'

Jack was very pleased with this.

So after the first week Jack went in, picked the best room he could get. Kindled a big fire and found the best bed he could pick in the big *bene cane*, big house. Jack was there for a week. Nothing happened.

But one night he was lying on the bed and dovering to sleep because he'd worked hard that day. He had a candle burning on the table. He was fully dressed. He never took his clothes off, just lying on top of the bed. Now the door led from where the bed was into a wee kitchen, where there was a back door. And Jack had left the door open going into the wee kitchen. Because it was warm now in the house Jack had opened the kitchen window to let some air in. And he was lying there after a good feed he had got from the old woman, braxy and tatties and everything. Baked scones and oh, he was really full up. He's lying in the heat there in the shadow o' the wee candle.

And he heard 'cluck-cluck, cluck cluck, cluck-cluck'. And he sat up in bed. 'Cluck-cluck, cluck-cluck.' And then coming walking in by the kitchen was a bonnie wee black hen. You know the hens with the silver earrings? Instead of their ears being red like any other hen's, they're silvery. Wee black hen not much bigger than a blackbird. A bit bigger than a crow. Anyway it came: 'Cluck-cluck-cluck-cluck-cluck.'

And Jack said, 'God bless my soul and body – a wee hen!'

He was glad to see the wee hen for company. And the hen – it jumped up on the bed beside him where he was lying. It cooried down.

'Cluck-cluck-cluck,' it closed its eyes and went to sleep.

Jack was dead tired. He was pleased and he stroked its back, the wee toy black hen. He stroked its back.

'Darling wee thing,' he says, 'keep me in company. I wonder where you've come from? Ay, you must have come down from the farm.'

But Jack stretched out, and there's the wee hen lying on the side of the bed in front of him. But then he must have dovered off to sleep somehow with his clothes on. And the next thing . . . he felt was . . . a hand rubbing his brow . . . a hand rubbing his brow. Jack sat up with fright.

'Don't be afraid,' a voice said. 'Don't be afraid, just lie still!'

But Jack couldn't lie still. The candle was still burning. And there lying on the bed beside him was the bonniest lassie he'd ever seen in all his life! Long, dark hair over her shoulders. A long, dark dress and her bare feet. He was dumbfounded.

He said, 'I'm sorry, my lady, I'm sorry!'

She said, 'It's all right. Lie still, lie still.'

But he said, 'I'm no in bed. I was just resting.'

She said, 'It's all right. It's all right, don't worry!'

But he said, 'Where do you come from, my dear? Am I intruding in your house?'

She says, 'Yes, it's my house. But just lie still!'

But Jack sat up. He said, 'I'll go if I'm bothering you.'

'No no,' she says, 'don't go! Just stay where you are. You're just a new arrival here, aren't you?'

'Aye,' he said, 'I've been here for about two weeks. And I'm working for old John and his old wife.'

'I know,' she said, 'they're relations of mine. Did anything disturb you?'

He said, 'Well, I'm looking . . .'

She said, 'What are you looking for?'

'I'm looking for the wee hen.'

'A hen?'

'Aye, a wee black hen that was in . . .'

And she smiled at him. She said, 'I'm the hen!'

'Na,' he said, 'you're not a hen! You're no a hen; you're a young lady!'

She says, 'Jack, I'm the hen. And Jack, I know about a lot o' things. Tell me why you're here.' So Jack told her the story.

'Well,' she says, 'Jack, look. I'll have to tell you my side o' my story. You see, my uncle was a magician. He and I used to travel into the East where he made a lot of friends, and he made a lot of money there. And I always wanted to come back here. I prayed and pleaded and begged for him to come back home, where I loved this house. This is my home. I was born here. And he said, *"You'll go back, but you'll not go as a human being. You'll go back as a hen! And you'll remain a hen. Only one hour of the night will you ever be yourself. Till some young man comes and takes you to the church and marries you as a hen!"* Now Jack, that's my story. He said, *"He'll have to love you and marry you as a hen before you ever receive your own form."'*

Jack was flabbergasted about this. He didn't know what to do. He said to himself, 'I couldn't make a fool of my father and mother, go back to my father and mother with a hen, tell them I'm going to marry a hen!' But the lassie was so beautiful and so nice.

There was an old clock on the wall. It went pong – one o'clock. The candle went out. It burnt down. And Jack got up, lighted another candle. And look . . . 'cluck-cluck-cluck,' sitting on the bed was the wee black hen.

'Ah,' Jack said, 'I fell asleep. What a dream I had. What a dream! Wasn't that a beautiful dream?'

But anyway, he couldn't help thinking about it the next day. It was a dream. It passed out, out of his mind. He worked hard all day. He spread dung on the fields. Garden work all day. But he sat with the old woman, sat and cracked, played a game of cards with the old man and did things till it was getting late. Nine o'clock, he bade the old couple good night.

He said, 'Ach well, I'll away down to my bed.'

But he didn't go to bed. He lighted a candle, kindled up the fire as usual. And stretched himself on the bed. He made no meat for himself, because he got plenty meat in the old house from the old folk. But the old clock, pong-pong-pong-pong . . . ten o'clock.

'Cluck-cluck, cluck-cluck, cluck-cluck,' in came the wee black hen again. Popped up on the bed beside him.

Jack said to himself, 'I wasn't dreaming. I couldn't have been dreaming! This must be happening really.'

But anyway he stretched out. He kind of dovered away. The wee hen's lying, he petted the hen lying asleep beside him. And then pong-pong-pong-pong, twelve o'clock went the clock. Wonst again he felt the bonnie hand, soft hand.

And Jack said, 'Oh, I must have fallen asleep.'

There was the young *bene mort* sitting aside him again. Same long black dress, same long black hair.

Jack said, 'It wasn't a dream!'

She says, 'What do you mean, Jack?'

He said, 'I thought I had a dream last night.'

She said, 'Jack, it's not a dream. It's all the truth. What are you going to do about it?'

Now the days had passed, the weeks had passed. Jack stayed in that house for three months and worked with the old folk. By this time ten months had passed since Jack had left his father and mother. And every night to Jack's enjoyment he couldn't wait, couldn't wait to get back! He wasn't doing half the work he should have done with thinking about the bonnie young woman. He finally made up his mind, if it was the last thing he ever did. He had to go back to his father in two months. Because the time would soon be up.

He said, 'Hen or no hen, I'm going to take the chance for it anyway. But I'll work away for a wee while yet.'

And the reason he worked was the enjoyment he had for an hour to spend with the young woman. He talked about many things. He tellt her about his brothers, and about his father. And she told him about the big house and how she owned it and all the money she had. And her uncle was gone for ever. He would never come back. He had mysteriously vanished. She tellt him all these stories.

At last one evening as he sat beside her when the clock struck twelve o'clock, she said, 'Jack, it'll soon be time.'

'What do you mean?' said Jack.

She said, 'In another month I'll have to be going back again to the East.'

'Ah,' says Jack, 'you're no going back; you're going with me!'

So the next morning he went up and tellt the old man and woman: he said, 'I have to go back to my father and mother.'

The old man and the old woman didn't want to see him go. They loved him like their own son.

She says, 'Look, when you go back, if you ever get a woman come back! Come back, Jack, laddie, come back!'

They loved him so much. By this time the old man's leg was a bit better. He could go about with a staff.

'Laddie,' he said, 'you saved my life. The wonderful things you've done for me. Please, please, Jack, come back!'

'Well,' Jack said, 'we'll have to wait and see.'

So that night he lay on the top of the bed as usual till the clock struck twelve o'clock. The wee hen had come in at ten. And at twelve o'clock the same thing happened – there was the young woman.

He tellt her straight: 'Look, tomorrow I must go.'

She said, 'Will you take me with you?'

'Well,' he said, 'there's nothing else for it.'

She says, 'Look, if you take me with you, you'd better watch me and be very careful with me, Jack. Because if a dog or cat or anything kills me, Jack, that'll be it finished. And I can't take back my form again till you marry me in church. And look on my foot. You'll see a ring.'

Jack looked. And there was a big silver ring on the wee hen's foot.

'Now,' she says, 'take it off, Jack, and keep it in your pocket and don't lose it!'

So then the candle went out once again. It got black dark and Jack fell sound asleep. He wakened in the morning and there was the wee hen coorying beside him.

So he packed all his wee bits o' belongings, went to the house and filled his pockets full of grain from the old farmer's shed. Bade the old man and the old woman goodbye, promised he would come back. Took the wee hen below his oxter and off he set.

He travelled on, sleeping in places here and sleeping in places there, giving the hen a wee taste of grain, feeding it and giving it a wee drink of water and taking good care of it. By the time he landed back at his father's farm one late evening the farm was in lunaries, lighted up! There were lights in every window, music playing, the old-fashioned gramophone was going.

Jack said, 'There must be a big party going on!'

The wee hen below his oxter, he walks into the great big sitting room of the farm. There was his father sitting by the fire, and his mother. Oh, his mother was in tears to see him back. He still kept his wee hen below his oxter. He put his one arm around his mother and he shook hands with his father. There sitting at the table were his two brothers with two beautiful young women.

Sandy had worked away with the farmer, fallen in love with the farmer's daughter. And the farmer had given Sandy his daughter to be married. Willie had worked away with the old cobbler, and the cobbler thought the world of Willie. Willie fell in love with the cobbler's daughter. And the cobbler gave Willie his daughter. Willie promised he would marry her and come back to the cobbler's shop. He'd have it to himself, because Willie had turned out to become a great cobbler, with him used to working in leather. Now they had everything they needed. All they needed was Jack. And they were waiting and this was when Jack walked into the farm house.

So after they all sat for a while the old farmer got out a bottle of whisky and passed it round. He was toasting them all.

He says, 'Jack, where's your bride? Your young lady?'

Jack said, 'Here – this is her!'

And Willie's future wife looked and she grunted her nose. And Sandy looked.

He said, 'But Jack, that's a hen!'

Aye,' he said, 'it's a hen and it's my hen. And tomorrow's the day, Father. Have you made arrangements?'

'Oh, of course we've got the arrangements. Everything's laid on for tomorrow. The carriage is coming for youse all. But where's your wife?'

He said, 'I tellt you, Father, this is my wife.' His mother thought Jack had went kind of droll.

But he said, 'Jack, that's only a hen, a wee black hen! A bonnie wee hen.'

Jack said, 'I'm marrying her tomorrow!'

Willie stood up. No,' he said, 'you're not going to church with me to marry a hen! No brother o' mine's going to marry a hen, not in the same church as me!'

Sandy said, 'No, no, I couldn't have it! My young brother marrying a hen in church – to get a name about us and shame us to death. I'm going back with my wife to her father when I'm married. We've got a good going farm o' wir own.'

Willie said, 'I've got a good going cobbler shop o' my own. And when we get married we want no disturbance. We want a good wedding. We want everybody happy. But you're not coming, Jack, not with that hen to the church!'

Jack said, 'It's my hen and I'm marrying her. Now I'm going to the church with youse.' But they argued and bargued.

But to keep peace the old woman said, 'It's your wee brother, you know, maybe he's kind o' droll – something wrong has happened to him.' The old woman was sad for her laddie Jack.

But anyway, Jack took good care of his wee hen that night and put it in the bed beside him. And the next morning, true to his father's word, the big carriage came to the farm door. And the whole village turned out. Because everybody in the village knew the farmer. He'd spent a lot of money in the village. He was a rich farmer. And they

knew the three laddies because they had all gone to the
village school. The old school master came and the minister,
and oh, everybody came! You know, the old trade farmers
and the whole village! Everybody came to the wedding.
And Sandy's bride's father was there, and Willie's bride's
father was there.

They marched the lassies down the aisle and gave them
away to the young men. And the minister said the sermon.
They were married.

Jack's father went up. He said: 'We've another marriage
coming up, Reverend!'

'Another marriage?' he said. 'Where's the young couple?'

'Jack, my young son Jack's getting married.'

Now everyone took their seats. And there Jack walked up
in front of the minister in the pulpit with the black hen. Wee
black hen below his oxter.

'Where's your bride?' said the minister.

Jack said, 'This is my bride.'

He said, 'I can't marry you to a hen!'

Jack said, 'You'll marry me to a hen! You're a minister,
aren't you? And you can perform marriage services, can't
you?'

'Of course,' he said, 'but not to a hen.'

Jack said, 'It's my hen and I want you to marry me to this
hen! I've got the ring in my pocket.'

And the father whispered in the minister's ear, 'Carry on!
Just to please him. Don't raise him up! He's my youngest son
and he's a wee bit queer in the head.'

'Anyhow,' said the minister, 'ladies and gentlemen, we
have another marriage to perform. And it's the queerest
marriage I've ever done in all my life.' Everybody was quiet
in the church. You could have heard a pin drop. 'This young
man is going to marry a hen.'

Willie's wife began to giggle on to her sleeve. And Sandy's wife began to giggle. Sandy gave her a dig with the elbow:

'Quiet,' he says, 'wait till you see this!'

So the minister says, 'Well, if we must perform the marriage, we must! Now, young man, name?'

He says, 'Jack.'

'Jack,' he said, 'you'll have to say these words after me. But what about your bride, your hen? It can't talk.'

Jack said, 'I'll talk for it. Don't worry about it, minister. Marry me to my hen! And I've got the ring.'

So the minister said, 'Ladies and gentlemen, we're here today to bind these two, these two – hen and man – together.' He couldn't say 'people'. 'Here to bind this hen and man for good or bad, in health, in sickness and in poorness.' Whatever they say, you know!

The minister says, 'Do you take this hen to be your lawfully married wife?'

And Jack said, 'Yes!'

'Well,' the minister said, 'have you got the ring?'

And Jack says, 'Yes!' And he put the ring over the wee hen's foot.

'To love and keep and hold and cherish for ever and ever and ever till death do you part?' said the minister.

Jack said, 'To love and hold and cherish and to keep till death do us part.'

He said, '*Now I pronounce you hen and husband.*'

And like *that* . . . a grey smoke arose where the wee hen was. And it got dark inside the church. People stood up and started to cry. But then as fast as the smoke came the smoke vanished. There beside Jack, standing with her arm linked to his, was the most beautiful young woman anyone had ever seen in all their life! Beautiful dark hair, long dark dress.

And Jack put his arms around her and he kissed her. The old farmer and the old wife didn't know what to do!

So that night they all met in the farmhouse and they had a great-going party. And usually when there are parties in the house and everyone's happy, someone has to tell a story. So Willie told his story and everybody listened about going to the cobbler. And Sandy told his story. But the most interesting story told that night was Jack's story, how he had met his wife, the wee black hen!

So the next morning after everything was squared up, Sandy said goodbye to his mother and father. He had a farm of his own; he didn't want his father's.

Willie said to his father, 'Father, it's no good to me. I'm going back to my cobbler shop. I'd rather have my shop.' He loved his cobbling shop.

'Well, Jack,' he says, 'you not only got the bonniest wife, you're entitled to the farm!'

Jack said, 'No, Father, it's no use to me. You keep it, Father! And when you retire, Father, sell it and give the money to the church to share among the poor folk. Because I'm not needing it!'

So the next day Jack and his young wife bade farewell to their mother and father. With a faithful promise the mother and father said they would come and visit, come and stay with Jack and his wife when they sold the farm. Because there was plenty of room in the big house.

And Jack went back to the big house with his young wife and there he stayed. He never needed to work because he had plenty, plenty money. But now and again he would always go with his friend the old farmer and give him a wee help. Because after all, he was suffering from a broken leg that was only newly mended!

That's old Willie Williamson's story. He was a cousin of my father's who stayed around Dunbartonshire, but always came to Argyllshire in the summertime. Across the burn from my father's barricade he would build his bow tents and fire. In the evenings we would sit and listen to his piping and singing and his great storytelling.

# The Beatin' Stick

Jack lived with his mother a long, long time ago. And his mother used to tell him all these wonderful stories at nighttime. Jack worked hard. He was a butcher by trade. He brought home plenty of meat to his mother, and they were well off. But one night he came home and brought plenty of food to his mother. And she was sitting. She seemed very downhearted.

He says, 'Mother, what's the trouble, what's wrong with you?'

'Well, son, I've been thinking. I've been thinking about my old sister.'

'Mother, your what?'

'My old sister, Jack – your auntie.'

'My auntie, Mother? I never knew I had an auntie.'

'Oh Jack, aye, my son, you've an auntie. And she's a long, long way frae here. I think she's no keeping very well. She's in trouble somehow.'

'Mother, how could you think that?'

'Well, Jack, you dinnae ken, it's a long story. Me and your auntie are twins, twin sisters. And she was forced to flee awa frae this country when she was young because people thocht she was working with the devil, *black art*.'

'Ah, Mother, there's nae such a thing as black art.'

'Ah well,' she said, 'she got the blame o' it. And folk was gaunnae burn her as a witch. She had to flee awa for her life!

And now I'm getting kind of worried about this. She must be coming up in years. And that's what I was gaunnae ask you, laddie. I ken you like your job with the butcher. But I would like . . . would ye do me a wee favour?'

'Mother,' he said, 'you know I'll do anything for you.'

She said, 'Ye ken I'm no bad off for money. You pay me well and I can manage myself. Would ye do your poor old mother a favour? Will ye gang and see your old auntie for me? And see how she's getting on.'

But Jack said, 'Mother, how can I go and see somebody I've never met, someone I didna even ken existed till this day?'

'Well, Jack, I didna want to tell you. I wanted to keep it secret from you because there's many bad names about your old auntie. And I didna want you to grow up with the thought that there was any trouble in the family.'

'Ah, but Mother, it's my auntie, isn't it? Your sister!'

'Aye, Jack, it's my sister. And she's the same age as me, Jack. She'll be seventy on her birthday and I've never seen her for forty years! And laddie, if you would gang and pay her a wee visit and tell her I'm all right, spend a wee time with her, come back and tell me how she's getting on – it would make me awful happy.'

'But, Mother, where does she stay?'

'Oh, Jack, she stays a long way frae here, a long, long way frae here! Away to the end of the land. The farthest point of Ireland, Jack, that's where she stays!'

'Oh well, Mother,' he said, 'you ken it's going to take me a long, long while and I cannae leave ye for as long as that.'

'Laddie, I'll be all right, Jack, when you're on your way. I ken naething'll happen to you. You go and see your old auntie and bring me back good news frae her. And if ever I die I'll die happy.'

So they sat and talked that night for a wee while. And Jack promised his mother he would go and see his old auntie. And this is where my story starts.

The very next morning Jack and his mother were up early. She made him a little breakfast and she fried him a wee bit collop. She made him a wee bannock to carry him on his way.

She says, 'Be careful, laddie, on your way! It'll maybe tak ye months, I dinnae ken. But it'll maybe tak ye weeks. But remember, I'll be always thinking about you. And may the best of luck gang with ye!'

Jack bade goodbye to his mother and off he set. Oh, Jack travelled on, and on and on asking people questions along his way, doing a wee bit job for these people here, doing a wee bit job for people there. He was in nae hurry. And he travelled on and on till he came to a long weary road. There were not a house in sight. And then he came down this steep brae.

There was a wee bridge crossing. He crossed the bridge and the first thing he saw was an old woman with a big bundle of sticks on her back. Oh, in the name of God, it was the biggest bundle Jack had ever seen an old woman carrying!

And he said to himself, 'How in the world can an old woman like that carry so many sticks on her back?' And he put on the speed and stepped quicker. He overtook the old woman.

He said, 'Old woman, how could you carry such a big bundle as that?'

'Ah,' she says, 'laddie, I'm carrying them but I'm getting really tired.'

'Well,' he said, 'let me take a wee shot frae you. I'm going on your way. Have you far to gang?'

'Aye,' she says, 'laddie, a wee bit yet.'

'Well,' he said, 'let me carry your sticks for you!'

And Jack being young and strong picked up the bundle and put it on his back. The old woman walked beside him and they travelled on for about a mile till they came to a wee thatched house by the roadside.

She said, 'Laddie, this is my house.'

And Jack could see there were heaps of sticks. The old woman had been carrying sticks, must have been carrying them for years!

But he said to her, 'What are you doing with so many sticks, old woman? You've nae need to carry so many as that. You've as much there that would keep my mother's fire burning for years!'

She says, 'I like to gather sticks. I love gathering sticks! And that's the only enjoyment I get out of life.'

He tellt her his name.

She said, 'Ye ken, Jack, sticks is a good thing. Let them be thorn sticks, jaggy sticks, hazel sticks, ash sticks, oak sticks. Any kind of sticks is good sticks!'

'Oh well,' said Jack, 'I suppose so.'

'Would you like to come in for a wee bit before you gang on your way?' she asked.

And Jack put the big bundle of sticks down beside the rest and the old woman brought him into this wee house. She made him something to eat and he sat and cracked to her. He tellt her where he was going.

She said, 'Laddie, you've a long, long way to gang, miles. It will tak ye weeks where you're gaun.' So she says, 'You've been good to me, laddie. Do you want to stay the night or do you want to gang on?'

'Ah,' Jack said, 'it's kind of early yet. I think I'll push on.'

So she gangs to the back of the door and pulls out a black-thorn stick. And there were more knots in thon stick than ever you've seen in your life! But it was polished like new mahogany.

She says, 'Jack, will ye tak this wi ye? Maybe you'll get tired on your way and it'll help you.'

But he said, 'I'm no an old man! I dinnae need a stick.'

She says, 'Jack, you might need this – because this is a different kind of stick from the stick you think it is. This might help you on your way. Jack, this is a magic stick!'

'Aye,' he said, 'old woman! There's nae such a thing as a magic stick.'

She said, 'Jack, this is a magic stick! You tak this stick frae me and on your journey back you can aye give it to me back. Will you do that for me?'

'Oh well,' says Jack, 'there's nae harm in taking a stick. It'll maybe help me along the road.'

But she says, 'If you're ever in trouble, you'll no need to worry about it. If onybody ever touches you or you're ever in trouble, just say, "*Stick, beat them*!" And then, Jack, you'll see that the stick is worthwhile o' keeping.'

Jack thought the old mort was kind of droll. But he took the old stick because he liked it. He'd never seen a stick like it before in his life. And he bade farewell to the old woman.

On he walked. And he travelled on and he travelled on. That night he slept under a hedge. And he had a perfectly good sleep with the stick in below his head! He had a wonderful dream.

So the next morning he set on his way and he travelled on. He was travelling down this kind of a forest when he hears all these funny noises and gibbling, gabbling, arguing coming from the back of the wood. Jack thought it was maybe people gathering for a kind of session or something. He wondered what was going on. He wanted to ask some questions from the folk where he was going.

And he came through a wee path in the wood through a clearing. In the clearing in the middle of this scrubby wood o' hazel trees he looked. He saw this band o' people. They were all gathered round in a circle.

Jack said, 'I wonder what's going on here.'

When he came in closer he could see there were three men on horseback, young men. Two o' them was dressed like soldiers. But the other one was dressed in these bonnie fancy clothes. They were surrounded by what Jack thought were robbers. Oh, some had patches on their eyes, ragged clothes, bare feet, trousers cut above their knees. They were a sorry-looking crowd. And some had crommacks in their hands. Some had kinds o' spears and some had knives. They were surrounding these three young men.

Jack said, 'They're robbin' some gentlemen!'

And he walked closer. They were pointing their sticks and spears at these three men on horseback.

Jack said, 'There's too many for me to start an argument. I wonder if that old woman is tellin the truth.' And he came in as close as he could. He held up this stick:

He said, '*Go on, stick, beat them!*'

Before you could say another word the stick flew from his hand. And that stick went straight for these robbers! Left and right went the stick cracking heads, breaking arms, cracking legs. Within minutes there wasn't a standing man in the whole place. And there stood the three horse-backed men by themselves. These robbers made off for their lives – those who were able to run! And them that weren't able to run lay on the ground moaning in pain. Jack went over and he picked up his stick. He walked up.

He said, 'Are you in trouble, sir?'

And this young gentleman on a horse said, 'Young man, where did you come from? I never saw anything so clever in all my life! You-you-you beat off fifty robbers!'

'Well,' Jack said, 'with the help of this! My stick.'

He said, 'I watched that stick. That's a clever stick! Where did you get it?'

Jack said, 'I got it from an old woman. And I promised to return it.'

'Well,' said the young man, 'do you know who I am?'

Jack said, 'No. Are you a gentleman or a laird o' some kind?'

He said, 'No, I'm the king!'

'The king?' says Jack. And he bowed before him and said, 'I'm sorry, my lord!'

'Don't bow before me, young man,' he said. 'What's your name?'

'My name is Jack and I'm going to the end of the land to see my old auntie.'

He said, 'Jack, before you go anywhere, clever young man, you must come with me and meet my family and meet my wife!

'Soldier,' he said, 'take Jack up with you on the back of your horse.'

So Jack was put on the back of the soldier's horse. And they rode on. After a few miles they came to this beautiful palace. The soldiers went one way with the horses and Jack and the king went right up the front steps into the most beautiful palace Jack had ever been in his life! The king clapped his hands. He called for footmen and maids to come and set a beautiful meal for Jack. And he and the king sat and they talked for a long, long time.

'Young man,' he said, 'Jack, I would like you to meet my queen. But to tell you the truth, she's not very well.'

'Oh,' says Jack, 'what's wrong with her?'

'Well,' he said, 'she has a problem. You see, my queen cannot sleep. She has never slept for many, many months.'

'Oh,' Jack said, 'that's terrible. She cannae sleep?'

He said, 'She's ill from the want of sleep, Jack. And the funny thing is, it all began a while ago when a young man tried to steal my fruit.'

Jack said, 'A young man tried to steal your fruit?'

'Oh, I forgot to tell you. Jack, you see my father, the king before me, had a wonderful fruit tree here. This is the Tree of Life, the Fruit of Life. And whoever feeds from that Tree of Life never takes ill. But we caught a young man stealing fruit from our tree. And naturally I had to send him to prison. From that day on my tree has never produced another fruit. And my wife has never had a wink of sleep.'

'Well,' Jack said, 'there must be something behind this. But I'll tell ye, I cannae stay to help you. I'm going off to see an old aunt o' mine. And my mother tells me she's very clever. I'll ask her when I go there and maybe she'll be able to help me.'

The king said, 'If ye can find ony help for me at all, Jack, I'll reward you handsomely when you come back. If you can find anything to help my tree and my queen I'll be much obliged to you, Jack!'

So the next morning the king ordered Jack a horse. He tellt Jack to go to the kitchens, get anything he wanted to carry with him. So Jack went to the kitchens and got some food. The king shook hands with him and told him when he returned he must come and see him – see if he could find an answer to his problem.

So, Jack with his stick under his arm and the bundle of food from the kitchen made on his way. He travelled on and on and on. To make a long story short, after a long, long time Jack came to where there was no more land; it was the raging sea.

And there at the end of the land at the seaside he came to a little cottage, a thatched little house. Hens running around, ducks swimming in the water, cocks sitting on the roof crowin.

Jack said, 'At last! This must be her.'

So he came in to the clearing and here he meets an old woman, the identical spit of his mother. Jack said, 'It's my mother!'

She said, 'Young man, I'm no your mother. Who are you?'

He said, 'I'm Jack. And I've come to see you. You're my auntie.'

'I'm your auntie?' she said.

'Aye,' he said, 'you're my mother's sister.'

'Oh laddie, laddie,' she says, 'you've come at last! I knew some day you would come.'

And she brought Jack into her little house. She fed him as best she could.

'Now,' she said, 'tell me about your mother.'

And Jack sat and he cracked to her and he tellt her about his mother. He tellt her about the journey he'd come, and he tellt her about his beatin' stick. He tellt her everything he could think of, everything since he was a wean. And she sat and listened to every word.

He said to her, 'Auntie, on my road here I had a funny experience. And only with the help o' my stick . . .' and he tellt her about the old woman giving him the stick.

The old woman looked at the stick. She says:

'Jack, that is a good stick. That is a real stick! You dinna ken the value o' that stick. But I ken.'

So he says, 'Auntie, will you tell me something? On my way here I ran into the king surrounded by a band of robbers,' and he tellt her the story. He tellt her about the king's wife who couldnae sleep. And he tellt her about the fruit tree.

'Aha, Jack laddie,' she said. 'Laddie, laddie, I ken you'll be wanting to go awa, but will you no stay with me for another two days? At least till I have a wee crack to you? I'm lonely here, I'm a lonely old woman here by myself. Can you no stay for another two days?'

'Well,' Jack said, 'I'll stay for another two days if you promise you'll answer me two questions!'

'Jack,' she said, 'if you stay with me two days I'll tell you onything!'

'Tell me then, why, Auntie, the king's wife the queen cannae sleep.'

'Aha, Jack, the king would gie the world to ken that!'

'And tell me, Auntie, why the king's fruit tree is no growing any more fruit.'

'Oho, Jack laddie, the king would give a large reward to ken that.'

'Well,' he said, 'what's the problem, Auntie?'

She said, 'It's the king's fault, Jack! If it wasnae his ain fault, it wouldnae hae happened. You see, he sent a young laddie to the dungeons for stealing the fruit of his tree. And that laddie's mother's a wee bit like myself, a wee bit o' the black art. And her daughter is working as a maid in the castle in the palace. Every night she combs the queen's hair and she puts knots in the queen's hair with the power of her old mother! And that's why the king's queen cannae sleep. She's also put her sword under the roots o' the king's tree. And that's why it's no growing ony fruit, Jack! That's the king's problem.'

So Jack was awfae pleased to hear this. He stayed another couple of days with his auntie.

And at last he said, 'Auntie, I'll have to go back to my mother. I've been away for a long, long while.' At least eight months had passed since Jack had left his mother, and he was dying to go back again. So he finally had to bid goodbye to his auntie.

And she said, 'Jack, you're only a young man yet. And promise you'll come back and see me again!'

'Well, Auntie,' he said, 'I might and I might not. Naebody kens that.'

'But give my best to your mother,' she said, 'my wee sister. And tell her I'm aa right, and I'm still surviving.'

And Jack bade his old auntie goodbye and took his wee stick under his arm. Away he set, back all the road home. He travelled on and on and on, and after nights and days had passed once again he was back at the king's palace.

He walked up the steps to the king's palace with his stick below his oxter. And the king was overjoyed to see him!

The king said, 'Jack, you've been away a long while. Come and have something to eat with me!'

So Jack dined with the king. He said, 'Jack, did you ever discover what I was telling you about? Did you ever find any answer for me?'

And Jack said, 'Aye. But listen! Look, you have a young man in prison and I want you to set him free. And you have a young maid who works for your queen. When I tell you the truth, will you promise me something?'

'Onything,' says the king, 'onything, I'll promise you! If my wife could get one night's peaceful sleep.'

And Jack said, 'You sent a young man to the dungeons for stealing your fruit.'

'That's true,' said the king.

And he said, 'His sister is your queen's maid.'"

'That's right,' said the king, 'but I didna ken it was *his* sister.'

'And every night,' said Jack, 'she combs your queen's hair. And her mother has a wee bit o' the black art.'

'Oh, I'll punish her,' said the king, 'I'll punish her!'

'No,' says Jack, 'you'll no punish her. Otherwise I'll tell you no more.'

'Come on then, Jack, tell me,' he said. 'And I swear I'll not do anything about it.'

So, Jack tellt the king. He said: 'You can sack her, send her on her way. And set the young man free.'

So, Jack tellt the king about the maid tying knots in the queen's hair. And the king ordered her away from the palace, and he set the young man free. Jack stayed that night with the king in the palace. And for the first time for many, many months the queen had the most beautiful sleep, the most beautiful sleep she had ever had!

'Now,' says the king to Jack, 'how about my tree?'

'Ah,' Jack said, 'that's simple. Come with me!'

Jack led the king down to the garden at the front of the palace, a beautiful garden of roses. And there in the middle of the garden was a tree completely withered. The leaves were dead, the branches were dead. And Jack reached, put his hand under the soil, under the roots of the tree. He pulled out a sword, a rusty sword.

And he said to the king, '*That* was the cause of your tree not bearing fruit.'

And within minutes the tree was blooming. All beautiful green!

The king scratched his head.

'Jack, Jack,' he said, 'I've never seen anything like this before in my life. I'm going to reward you more than ever you'll need.'

But Jack said, 'I've a long way to go and I cannae carry very much.'

The king said, 'Well, Jack, you can fill your pockets, can't you?'

So, Jack filled his pockets with gold from the king and he bade the king farewell. He went on his journey.

He travelled on and he travelled for a couple of days. It was gloamin dark when he saw a wee light by the roadside.

'Aha, at last,' he said, 'I'll have a rest tonight.'

He walked to the door and knocked. And an old woman opened the door to him.

She said, 'Who are you there? Who is it here this time of night?'

And Jack said, 'I've brung back your stick!'

'Oh, come in laddie,' she says, 'come in!'

And Jack spent a lovely evening with the old woman. He had a nice long talk to her and a lovely supper with her. And he had a good sleep. In the morning he bade her farewell. But before he left he held out the stick.

He said, 'Here's your stick! Take your stick back.'

'Nah, nah, Jack,' she says. 'I'm no taking the stick back, laddie. You keep the stick! Because some day I might need you to carry me another bundle of sticks and you never know – maybe the king will have another task for you!'

Jack bade the old woman goodbye and he walked home. And after a few days' travelling he landed back to see his old mother.

She was overjoyed to see him. And he came in.

She says, 'Jack, did you mak your way, laddie?'

'Oh, Mother, Mother,' he said, 'ye've nae idea – have I got a story to tell you!'

And Jack had a wee cup o' tea, and he sat down by his mother. He placed his wee stick by the fire. He tellt his mother the story. And the story he tellt his mother is the one I've tellt you right now!

That was Old Toots's story, old Johnnie MacDonald. He was an old Travelling man called 'The Story Mannie' by children in Aberdeenshire. Oh, I was only about eighteen when he told me it. We were staying up near CouparAngus. I've told it since then among Travellers, just among Travellers.

# Jack and the Devil's Gold

Jack was reared with his old mother. They lived in this cottage and everything she done was just for the sake o' getting him reared up the best she could.

But one morning she says to him, 'Jack, ye'll have to gang to the town and get two-three bits o' messages today again.'

'I dinna mind goin for the messages, Mother; but look, can ye gie me a shilling to myself?'

'What are ye wantin a shilling for?'

'Ye ken what I want a shilling for – to get a wee bit *thing* to myself.'

'Look, bad luck's going to follow you yet,' she said, 'ower the heids o' this drink, this carry-on. Drinkin is goin to get you into serious trouble.'

He says, 'Mother, for all the drink that I get it'll no do me much harm.' But anyway, he hemmed and hawed and he managed to beg her for half a crown to go to the town.

'Now,' she says, 'remember, I ken that you're goin to come back the shortcut through the wood. And Jack, if it's late, dinna come back through there! I tellt ye an awfa bing o' times, 'cause I'll tell ye something: some o' these times the Devil'll get ye comin back through the shortcut!'

Now, where Jack stayed in this wee house with his mother, if he went round the road it was about two miles to the wee village. But if he came back through the wood by the shortcut he had to pass this big clift in this rock. And it was a dreary path through the wood.

But away Jack went to the town and he bought his two-three bits o' messages for his mother, whatever he needed. And in to the pub, he spent his half-crown. And he got hisself a good-goin drink. By the time he got out o' the pub it was about ten o'clock. He got his mother's wee bit messages on his back. And he went back the road.

But when he came to the crossroads he said, 'Man, it's a long bit round about that road. There naethin's goin to bother me goin through this shortcut.'

His mother had warned him not to take it at night. He went it two-three times during the day. He kent it, knew the road well. But he'd never come through it at night before. It was ten' o'clock, the month of October and the moon was shining clearly. And with the drink in his head he said, 'Ach, I canna walk that bit the night. I'm going back through the shortcut.'

So back he comes. And he travels on, he travels on. But before getting near the house he had to come to a bad bend in the road. And there was a face o' a clift. Then there was the path that led ye down to the house. The moon was shining clear. Jack's walking on the wee pad and he's dottering on, ye ken, a wee drink on him! And he looks – lyin right on the pad shinin – a gold sovereign. Jack bends and he picks it up, brother, and he looks.

'Oh dear-dear,' he says, 'if I'd hae come this way the first time I could hae haen that. I could hae haen that drunk. But it'll keep to the mornin.'

But he'd only taken another two steps ... another yin! And after he'd taken another step – another one! But these coins weared away up the pad. And he followed them, he picked them up as he went.

He came to the face o' the clift. He looked: there was a dark hole and he could see a light. A light, and he seen a fire shinin in a monster cave in the face o' the clift!

He says, 'I never kent this place was here before. Maybe it's an old buck gadgie with a fire. Maybe he's lost his money, maybe he stole it fae somebody. He dropped it from a hole in the bag or something. He's in there wi all that loor. Tsst, I'm goin in for a crack to him, maybe he's got somethin to drink!'

He walks in, into the face o' the clift. He sees this big fire and here this man's sittin. Tall dark man sittin at the fire.

'Come on, Jack!' he said. I've been waitin for you for a long, long while, Jack, come on in!'

So Jack walked further in. But a funny thing about the fire was, the sticks was burning but they werena seemin to be deein out. Shadows was round the wall, Jack could see the shadows of the fire was making droll faces on the front of the wall.

The man says, 'Sit down, Jack.'

Jack sat down.

The man says, 'Ye never done what yer mother tellt ye, did ye?'

'No,' says Jack, 'I never done what my mother tellt me.'

He said, 'Yer mother tellt ye not to come back the shortcut tonight, didn't she?'

'Aye,' said Jack, 'but if I hadna come back I wouldna hae found the money.'

'What money did ye find, Jack?'

'I found money on the road up. And it led me into this cave. You stole it and you lost it. It's mine now! You stole it fae somebody.'

He said, 'How much did you get?'

Jack said, 'I got a good few onyway.'

Hand in his pocket, brother, nothing! Not a haet. He emptied his pocket outside in – nothing!

And this man laughed: 'Na, na, Jack,' he said, 'ye mightna look in yer pocket, laddie, there nothing in yer pocket. Ye like money, Jack, don't ye?'

'Aye,' said Jack, 'I like money. I was reared with my mother since my father dee'd. I dinna remember much about him. And me and her got a hard time o' it.'

And he said, 'Ye like a drink, Jack?'

'Oh-oh, I like a drink all right, I love a drink.'

'And you spend every wee copper that yer mother's got for the sake o' buyin drink. And she's to do wantin a lot o' things that she could buy for the money you spend.'

Jack said, 'That's got nothin to do wi you.'

He said, 'Jack, that's got an awfa lot to do wi me! Look, if you want money, there a boxful there, help yersel! Take as much as ye want.'

Now, when Jack sat with his mother at the fire in their house, it was a peat fire they had. And Jack used to be fond o' sittin at the fire with his bare feet. They always used to keep a creel o' peats at the fireside. When the fire burnt down Jack would be lyin back gettin a good heat, his mother used to tell Jack to put a bit peat on the fire. And he could bend down, he could lift a peat with his toe and put it on the fire with his foot, his bare foot – to save him from getting up – touch o' laziness, ye see! And Jack had practised this for years and he'd got that good at it. Well, Jack was as clever with his foot as he was with his hand.

So the Devil said, 'There's plenty in the box, Jack, help yerself.'

So Jack put his hand in the box, lifted it up, a handful. Then, two hands. When he got it in his two hands . . . dust, brother, dust! The man looked at him and he laughed.

Jack said, 'In the name of God, who are you? You're bound
to be the Devil!'

He says, 'Jack, that's who I am; I'm the Devil.'

'Well,' Jack said, 'look, if you're the Devil, that's Devil's
money. And it's nae good to me.'

'Oh aye, Jack,' he said, 'it's good to you, Jack. You can have
as much o' it as you can tak. *But you've got to tak it the way
that I canna tak it.*'

Jack looked down and he seen the cloven foot sittin, the
right foot, split foot. Jack said, 'If I can lift it the way you
canna lift it, can I keep it?'

'That's the bargain, Jack!' he said.

Jack says, 'Right.'

Slipped off his old boot, brother, off with his old stocking.
He lifted the lid of the box. Jack put the foot into the box,
with his two toes he lifted a gold piece and he put it in his
hand. There it was shiny as could be. He put it in his pocket.
Another yin. And another yin, till he had about forty. Weight
in his pocket.

'Now,' he says to the Devil, 'you do the same for me!'

Devil put the . . .

'No,' says Jack, 'the same foot as me – the *right* foot – get
it in the box and get them out!'

Devil put the cloven foot into the box, brother. He tried
with the split foot, but na – ye're wise!

He says, 'Jack, ye finally beat me!' And just like *that* there
were a *flash o' flame*, brother dear. And darkness.

Jack rubbed his eyes, he wakened up. He was sitting with
his back against the clift, sober as a judge against the clift.
And the clift was closed, not a soul to be seen. He got up,
lifted his mother's wee bundle and he walked home. He
landed in. His old mother was sitting in the house.

She said, 'Ye're hame, Jack.'

He said, 'Aye, I'm hame.'

She said, 'Did ye get a wee drink?'

'Drink! Mother, I got mair than a drink . . . I got the biggest fright I ever got in my life.'

'What happened?'

'I met the Devil!'

'Aye,' she says, 'you met the Devil!'

'Aye, I met the Devil,' and he told her the story I'm telling you. 'But Mother, I beat him, I beat the Devil. He couldna do what I done. You used to cry me, Mother, a lazy cratur when I was sittin at the fire puttin peats on the fire wi my feet.'

'Aye,' she said, 'naebody would put peats on with their feet. It's only *you*, a bundle of laziness!'

'Well,' he said, '*that's* no a bundle o' laziness – forty gold sovereigns in my pocket. The Devil couldna lift them with his right foot, but I beat him when I lifted them with mine.'

Jack and his mother had forty gold sovereigns and they had a good time o' it. All because he put the peats in the fire with his foot!

# The Tramp and the Farmer

It was very late when the old beggar-man came to the rich farmyard. He had travelled far that day, he was tired and hungry.

He said to himself, 'I must find somewhere to sleep', because it was snowing. There were many buildings in this farm by the side-road. He said, 'I will go up here, maybe the farmer will help me. He has many barns, he has many sheds. He could probably give me somewhere to lie down.'

So the old beggar-man walked up to the farmhouse and he knocked on the door.

The farmer was just after finishing his tea, and his wife said, 'There's someone at the door.'

And the farmer said, 'Well, I'll go and see who's there.'

He walked out and there at his door stood an old beggar-man with his old grey hair and his old ragged coat. He had travelled for many miles.

And the farmer said, 'What do you want, old man?'

He said, 'Please, sir, I'm just an old beggar. Would you please, could you help me?'

'What do you want of me?' said the farmer.

'Look, just a shed, or a barn or any place you could let me lie for the night. It's a cold night and it's snowing. I'm hungry and tired, but just a place to lie down would be enough for me for the night, just some place to shelter.'

And the farmer said, 'You're a beggar! Old man, I need my barns for my cattle. The woods are fit for you. Go and sleep in the wood, old man, we shelter no beggars here. My barns are for my cattle, not for you, old beggar-man. Go and sleep in the wood! This is not for you.'

The old beggar just turned around. He said, 'I'm sorry, sir.' And he walked away.

The farmer closed his door.

But the courtyard of the farm was a big yard. And there were two ways leading from the yard; the road leading up to the farm and the road leading away from the farm. The old beggar walked among the snow coming down. And who at that moment was coming out from a shed but the farmer's coachman!

In these days it was all horses and coaches, and there was a special shed made for the coaches. The man was just after cleaning up the farmer's coach, his special coach that took him to the village and to the town. He had put the coach in the shed. And when he walked out the first person he met was the old beggar-man, who was walking down through the farmyard.

The coachman said, 'Where are you going, old man?'

And the old beggar said, 'I was up at the farmer, son. I was lookin for a shelter for the night, an' I asked him to let me sleep in the barn or any shed he had, any shed, just for shelter from the snow. And he told me to go and sleep in the woods.'

'Oh-oh,' said the coachman, 'you cannot sleep in the woods, old beggar-man. It's too cold tonight. Let me help you.'

'Your master will be angry,' said the old beggar.

'Never mind my master!' said the coachman. 'Come with me, one place I will take you to where he will never find you. Come into my coach shed. I have just cleaned up the farmer's coach. Come with me, old beggar, and the farmer will never find you there!'

And he took him into the coach shed, he opened up one of the farmer's prize coaches.

He said, 'Old beggar-man, it is comfortable in there. Go to sleep in there. Be out early in the morning and no one will ever know you've been there.'

So he put the old beggar in and he closed the door – a beautiful leather coach, all done up in beautiful leather. And the old beggar-man stretched himself out and went to sleep. The coachman went home to his wife and family.

The farmer inside the house went to bed. He went to sleep. But as he lay in bed and went to sleep he had a dream. He dreamt that he died and he went to Hell. And when he landed in Hell all the people that he knew in his lifetime, who had died before him, were all sitting around waiting their turn.

There was the Devil standing with a big pot of boiling lead and a ladle in his hand. And all the people round, all whom he had known who had died and he'd met in the market many years before, farmers he had known for many years, were all sitting around waiting their turn. One by one they were called up and the Devil took a ladle of boiling lead. They opened their mouths and they swallowed it. They were suffering in pain and they called in pain. One by one, till it came his turn.

And the Devil beckoned him up: 'Come, farmer, it's your turn next!' And the Devil put the ladle in, in his pot of lead and said to the farmer, 'Open your mouth – it's your turn.'

The farmer opened his mouth and the Devil put a ladleful of boiling lead in his mouth. And he felt it going down in his throat, it was burning him, burning in his throat and it was burning in his chest. And he said, 'Oh! Oh God, what have I done for this? If only I had one sip of water to cool my mouth!'

Then he looked up. And there came an old beggar-man with two brass cans of water before him. He stood before the farmer.

The farmer said, 'Please, I beg of you, please, old beggar-man, please, please! I beg of you, please, my mouth is burning, my throat is burning. Please give me one . . . even put your finger in, put one dreep on my tongue to cool my mouth!'

The old beggar-man said, 'No! My master forbids me. I cannot give you one sip. No more than you could give me one night's sleep in your barn.' And then the old beggar-man was gone.

'Oh-o-oh,' said the farmer, 'what have I done for this? Please, what have I done for this?'

And then he wakened up in his bed. 'Oh! Oh God,' he said to himself, 'what have I done? That old beggar that's in . . . that old beggar is probably in my barns, probably he's smoking, probably he's lightin his pipe an settin my barns on fire!'

He got up from his bed. He walked round all the sheds on his farm. But he never saw the old beggar. Then he saw a light in the coach house. He walked down, an' he opened the door of the coach house.

Then he walked into the coach and he saw the old beggar lying there – *four hands holding two candles each beside the old beggar's head and at his feet*. And the farmer was aghast. He walked back, backwards from the shed.

He said, 'It's the old beggar and he's dead.'

He walked home, he went to his bed. But he never had another dream.

Next morning when he got up he called for the coachman. The coachman came before him.

He said, 'Coachman, did you let an old beggar in my coach last night?'

The coachman said, 'Yes, master. You can sack me if you want to. I don't care. You can have my job. But I could not let an old beggar lie asleep in the snow.'

And the farmer said to him, 'Sack you, my man? I'm not going to sack you in any way. I'm going to make you manager of my farm and everything I own. You can work it for me for the rest of your life. Tomorrow morning I want you to go down to the joiners and get a beautiful sign made telling the world – TRAMPS AND BEGGARS WILL BE WELCOME – and a bed and whatever they can eat. Put it at my road-end. And you can run the farm for me for the rest of my time.'

So the coachman got that done. He put a sign on the road-side at the farm saying, TRAMPS AND BEGGARS WILL BE WELCOME. But the farmer waited, and he waited and he waited for many, many years. Never a tramp or a beggar ever came to his doorway until the day he died.

And what happened to that farmer I'm sure you know as well as what I do.

# Johnny McGill and the Crow

Johnny McGill is a legend in the West Coast and many parts of Scotland forbye. But he was a great friend of the farmers, so let me tell you . . . My father used to sit at night-time and tell us stories in the tent away back home in Argyll when we were small and sometimes we would bring up the subject of Johnny McGill, whom he knew personally well back in the thirties; because my father had camped with him, and so had many of the Scottish Travelling folk, especially in Argyll, not so much in Perthshire. And of course they had strange stories to tell. Because Johnny McGill had came out of nowhere. He had a little handcart painted green that said FROM LAND'S END TO JOHN O' GROATS TEN TIMES ON FOOT. He and his wife Mary didna have any children.

But the thing that disturbed most of the Travelling people at that time was the material that Johnny McGill carried with him; there were bottles and packages and things that he kept separated from his foodstuffs and other things because Johnny McGill at heart was a vet. Nobody knew where he came from. He was married to a Traveller woman, and of course the local Travelling women at that time always kept in contact with old Mary, because she saved up clothes for the children and she gave them things and she always had money when they had nothing. So they had no disrespect for old Mary; I think she was a McGregor.

But Johnny McGill had come out of nowhere, as I said. It was all right around the campfires, the Travellers would crack to him, they'd come over to him, but they had this thing in their head that he was a kind of a student or a kind of doctor that would get in touch with ... because the burkers were in strong force at that time, and burkers were never far from the Traveller's mind, the body-snatchers! ... Johnny McGill was a kind of an agent for the burkers and this was just a front, this vet carry-on. But he was a great favourite with the farmers. And of course his name was well known on the West Coast.

So my story begins. One of Johnny's stories begins in Argyll in Kilmichael Glassary. Between Kilmichael and Kilmartin there's a little quarry where the Travellers used to stay. And of course a group of the Travellers was there in that quarry, my father included. Now Johnny McGill was, I say, a collector, not of any collectable material, but he liked to collect any kind of little animal that was hurt – frogs that were trampled on with horses, rabbits that were hurt with an old-fashioned car of some kind. He was even known to carry a deer on his little cart because it was hit and needing mended. Crows, jackdaws, pigeons – all the little animals. And when he was settled for a wee while, him and old Mary, farmers who knew of him would come and get in contact with him if they had a sick animal, he'd go along to them. And he became well known.

But anyway, there was a group of Travellers camped in the quarry in Kilmichael Glassary many years ago, just shortly after the 1914 war, and of course people were very strict about the Travellers in those days. The local police moved them on, they were a kind of a menace, they were beggars, they werenae thiefs, but they got the name of being thieves and children stealers, you know, all these things said about the Travelling People. But actually they were honest, hard-working people. And of course the local landowners when they were pitched on their land, the first thing on their mind was to move them on to someone else's property.

So this group of Travellers was camped in Kilmichael Quarry, which I've camped in many times myself, when the local landowner's wife came along on horseback. And she saw this group of Travellers camped in the quarry, and she thought to herself, this is my husband's property. Why do these people be in there in this place anyhow, what are they doing there? She knew, passed down, all the Travellers were thieves and children-stealers, and at night when people were sleeping they would steal and thieve. Which was just a lot of nonsense! But she had this belief in her head.

So she dismounted from her horse and she came over. She said, 'What are youse people doing here?'

And a few of the women came up and said, 'We're resting, we're camped here, this is an old traditional . . .'

'This is not a traditional camping place; this is my husband's property!' And of course she came down off her horse and she lectured away to the Travelling people, told them they must move on, she would call the police, you know, naturally call the police, carry on, you must go on! And after a good lecture she mounted her horse and rode back. The Travellers paid no attention to her, she was just another woman.

But anyhow, it was summertime, in the late evening who should come along but her husband on the same horse! And when he came to the Travellers, he said, 'I thought my wife had told you to move on this morning?'

And someone of the Travellers said, 'We've things to do and we can't move. We'll move when we feel like it.'

But he said, 'Look, I'm not so much worried about you moving on, but I was wondering if any of you had seen a ring? My wife was along here this morning.'

'Oh,' they said, 'yes, your wife was along here and she gave us a lot of cheek and chat, you know.'

'Well, she lost her wedding ring and it means so much to her.'

And camped close to the side of the road was Johnny McGill with his wife Mary and his little tent. And Johnny had rescued a crow, a black crow that had a broken wing. And he had carried it with him on his little cart for days and weeks. And he'd mended its wing the best he could but it still couldnae fly. And it became a kind of a pet with him, and it would hop around the fire, it was a novelty for the children. Johnny McGill's crow!

The landowner said, 'Look, I'm no worried about you moving on, but I'm more worried about my wife's ring. She's lost her ring.'

And then out from the crowd of Travellers, men standing around the fire, Johnny McGill stepped and he said to the man, 'Sir, if I was you, I wouldn't be riding that horse.'

And the young laird says, 'Excuse me, what did you say?'

He said, 'Sir, if I was you I wouldn't be riding that horse.'

'What's wrong with the horse?' he said. 'It's my horse, it's my wife's horse.'

'Well,' he says, 'if I was you, I'd be more careful!'

He said, 'What do you mean, man?'

He said, 'Your horse is lame in the front left foot.'

Said, 'There's nothing wrong with my horse's left foot.'

'There's something serious wrong with your horse's foot and it's going to get worse, and,' he says, 'can you excuse me a moment.' And he walked over and he picked up the horse's foot and he looked at it. He says, 'Where did you get your horse shod last?'

He said, 'Of course my local blacksmith shoes my horse for me.'

'Well,' he says, 'eh, it wasn't the local blacksmith that done that.'

'No, in fact, it wasn't,' he said, 'it was the apprentice – the boy!'

'Well, I'll tell you something,' he said, 'the apprentice made a big mistake. One of the nails in your horse's shoe is piercing the quick of your horse's foot, and I would get it removed immediately if I was you!'

'What do you know about this?' said the young laird, 'What's your name, old man?'

He said, 'My name is Johnny McGill.'

'Oh! This is Johnny McGill. Yah, I've heard about you,' he said, 'I've heard about you from some of my friends. You're supposed to be a vet.'

'Well,' Johnny said, 'they say that, but if I was you, sir, I would get that shoe removed as soon as possible. One of the nails is piercing the quick of your horse's hoof, it's been drawn too close to the hoof by the apprentice, and I would get it removed immediately if I was you.'

And the laird turned round, he said, 'Could you remove it for me?'

Johnny McGill said, 'Of course I could remove it for you. But I'll remove it on one condition, you walk it home!' And he went into his tool box and he took out a pair of grips, things that he used for the material, and within seconds he removed the horse's shoe. 'Now,' he says, 'walk it home! And, I think this belongs to you,' and he handed the laird's wife's ring to the laird.

And the laird looked at it, and 'Where in the world,' he said, 'did you get that?'

Johnny says, 'I got it from my crow, that little fellow there, that little fellow picked it up this morning.'

And the laird said to him, 'Listen, pay no attention to my wife! My wife was along here this morning. But she'll be more than delighted to receive her ring back. And I'm more than delighted to know that my horse will be . . .'

'On one condition,' says Johnny McGill, 'that you don't go on its back for the next three or four days to come, but leave it running around in the field! And don't shoe it again for another week.'

And the laird turned round, he said, 'Let me tell you something, youse people; you stay here, as long as you want, and if anybody bothers you again, send them to me!' And the laird led his horse away. And the next morning the Travellers were gone. They were all gone.

And it was the laird passed by in his old car, and he stopped, and he said, 'These strange, strange people! You tell them to move and they stay, and you tell them to stay and they're gone.'

Now these were the stories of Johnny McGill, and of course he was a legend in his own time. But the Travellers were a wee bit eerie of him because of all the stuff he carried, but some of them began to understand; it took them a long, long time to really understand Johnny McGill, and these are the stories my father used to tell us in the tent a long time ago. Many, many wonderful stories, personal experiences from Johnny McGill because he knew him. And then, he was gone! His voice was gone as if he'd never existed, but his stories are still with us today after all those years. And that's the truth about Johnny McGill, so if ever you tell one of his stories, remember you're telling a story about something that really took place a long time ago.

## Blind Man and his Dog

Now, there's a story that goes down through history. And I mean people have seen the ghosts of animals – as well as the ghosts of humans. Many people have claimed to have seen a black dog, a black horse. But you don't know. If a person says to you, 'I saw a ghost', you cannae say he never seen a ghost! Five thousand people have said they saw something that represented a Loch Ness monster. How are we to say that they didn't see something that they thought was the Loch Ness Monster? I mean, five thousand folk, and among these people were some honest, good-living, hard-working people. Doctors, ministers, lawyers of all description, and they maintained they saw something.

If somebody says to you they saw a ghost, probably they did – what they thought was a ghost. So, I'm going to tell you a story.

There wonst lived an old brother and sister. And his name was Donald MacDonald – but no relation to John MacDonald the Traveller, because he was a shepherd. He was a good shepherd and he worked for a local farmer with his dog. And his dog's name was Bob. He loved Bob, since he was a wee pet; Bob was the love of his heart. His old sister Mary had never married, she stayed with them in their little cottage.

But then the sadness was, his lovely dog died. Bob died. And when Donald retired, something terrible happened,

because he went blind, completely blind. And of course
Mary took good care of him every way she could. She gave
him everything his heart desired. But he always had one
thought in his mind: Bob, his old dog.

So in October month, across the hillside from the cottage
where he lived, there was a group of hazel trees. And his
sister Mary had a great love for wild hazelnuts. Every year
in the time when he had his sight, that was the time he
would gather wild hazelnuts for Mary, bring two big pokes
of hazelnuts back for her. 'Specially round Hallowe'en time.

So now that he was blind, he wasn't a shepherd anymore
and his old faithful dog was gone, all he could do was sit by
the fireside waiting on Mary to do all the things for him.

One afternoon she comes into him and she says, 'Donald,
I'll have to go to the village. And the weather's not very
good.' She says, 'It's coming up for Hallowe'en and I'll have
to get some stuff in for Hallowe'en in case we get any visitors, kids come, you know, to the house. I won't be long.' She
had a little bike she cycled to the village, her bike.

But anyway, he thought about this. Now, he's blind. But
he knew that way to the trees. And he thought to himself . . .
with his stick he would surprise Mary. He would make his
way to the trees even though he was blind – he knew that in
his mind, how he would do it. And there was a gate that led
to the field. Under this gate it was wet, and there were a
fence along, towards the hill trees.

He said, 'If I get through the gate and get my hand on the
fence and follow the fence along till I get to the trees, I'll
manage to get a pocketful of nuts and surprise Mary when
she comes back even though I'm blind.'

So he got up with his walking stick. He was away through
the door and he walked down tapping here and there with
his stick. He felt the wet behind his knees, below his feet, he

knew he was at the gate. And he put his hand on the fence and he followed the fence along. He made his way towards the trees. But he could not reach up into the trees. He groped on his knees on the ground and all the nuts had fallen from the trees. Soon he filled his pockets.

But unknown to him the farmer had come and put some cattle in the field and closed the gate, the gate where the mud goes through. Where he went through – he knew it was a muddy place.

So the mist came down. It was a cold night, and he tried to find his way back but he got completely lost. He got lost.

Mary came back from the village. She searched for him, she couldn't find him. And the mist came down. She didn't know where he was. So naturally she had to go down to the local police and report him missing.

'Well,' the police said, 'we cannae dae nothing till the mist clears. We'll go out a search party on him when the mist clears.'

But now, Donald is sitting there wondering where in the world he is. He can't make his way back, he's completely lost. When all in a minute he felt a cold nose on his hand. And he put his hand up and he felt . . . 'Bob!' he said, 'Bob! He's come back to me.'

He put his hand round the neck and he felt the collar and he felt the collar tag, and he knew that tag well. And then he put his hand on the collar and it began to pull. He stood up.

And he said, 'Bob, take me home! Take me home, Bob.'

The dog led him as if it were a blind dog, a blind person's dog. It led him back to the gate and he reached up. He felt the gate, he opened the gate. And he closed the gate behind him. And the dog led him right to the door of his house. He walked into the house with his pocketful of nuts and there was Mary waiting on him.

She says, 'Where have you been, Donald?'

He said, 'I went to get you some nuts.'

She said, 'The police are looking for you, I reported you to the police! You've been missing for hours. How did you get back,' she says, 'in the mist?'

'Well,' he said, 'mist means nothing to me; I can't see any mist.'

'Well,' she said, 'they're going to put a search party out for you when the mist clears. How did you get home?'

He said, 'Bob brought me home!'

'Bob brought you home?'

'Of course,' he said. 'Bob came to me where I sat at the hazel trees. He sniffed my hand with his wet nose. And I felt his collar and he led me back.'

She said, 'You've been dreaming.'

'No, I've not been dreaming. I told you, Bob took me back all the way. Right to the gate,' he says, 'someone closed it. But I opened it and closed it again.'

She said, 'There's no way – the dog's been dead for years.'

He said, 'Bob took me home, I'm telling you! He took me back to the door of the house.'

But she wouldn't believe him. The next morning when the mist cleared she knew no one had come through that mucky gate but himself, and she walked down and she found her brother Donald's footsteps in the mud. And by his side was the footsteps and paw marks of a dog, by his side. And she knew that Donald was telling the truth. For the ghost of Bob had come back and taken his old master home to the house. She never argued with him again when he mentioned Bob.

And that is a true story.

# A Present for Grandmother

A long time ago away in the far north of Scotland in a little village there lived a little girl called Jenny Weir. Jenny's mummy and daddy had been drowned in a boating accident when she was only two years old. And Jenny went to live with her grandmother. Her granddad was an old roadman who took care of the roads. They were very, very poor. In those bygone days wages were very small. Old Granny took care of Jenny even though her heart was broken to lose her only daughter. Jenny was her only grandchild.

Little Jenny went to school in the local village. The little house where they lived was not far from the village. But on the way to school there was an old castle that dated back before time.

And Granny had always warned Jenny when she travelled to school, 'Jenny, please don't go near the old castle because the people say it's haunted. And if you go near that castle, you never know what might happen to you!'

And Jenny said, 'Oh Granny, I'll not go near the castle. I promise you!'

Jenny was very happy with her granny. And the people of the small village knew Jenny very well; they called her 'Little Jenny'. They felt very sad for her because she had lost her parents.

And then for some strange reason her granddad took sick, and after a short illness her granddad was gone. Jenny was sad to lose her granddad, for she loved him very much. He had told her many stories, stories about the old castle. He said it was haunted: there was an old woman who wandered the castle; she was the guardian of the castle. Jenny was always a little scared, even in daytime when she passed by the ruins of the old castle. And she remembered her grandmother's words . . .

Jenny's granny was very poor. She only lived on her pension. And a pension in these bygone days was not very much, about five shillings a week. Granny tried very hard to stitch and sew and mend, do things for Jenny to bring her up the best she could. Jenny loved her grandmother very, very much.

But one day just two weeks before Christmas Jenny travelled off to school with a little bag on her back. She'd only about a quarter of a mile to go. She passed the castle, and as she looked up she saw something very beautiful. For high on the castle was a holly tree. It was in full bloom with all those beautiful red berries.

And she thought, 'Where am I going to get a present for Grandmother? It will soon be Christmas. There's nothing to get. I have no money and Grandmother can't afford to give me anything.'

But Grandmother had warned her, 'Keep away from the old castle, Jenny. It's haunted.' Jenny was scared.

Then she said, 'I must find a present for Grandmother!' Where could she find one?

Soon it was just three days before Christmas. Jenny started home that afternoon from school. But she thought and stopped:

'There's nothing in that castle to scare me. It's only an old ruins, just some walls. And that beautiful little holly tree up there has all these wonderful red berries. Wouldn't it be nice if I could take Grandmother some holly as a little present?' So finally she said, 'I'll do it! I'll climb the wall. Grandmother will never know. I'll get her some holly.'

So she left her little school bag down by the ruins that led to the old castle. And she walked in, over the old stones that had fallen from the walls. She climbed up and up the wall. The holly tree was right on the top of the castle, just a small tree. And the berries were red hanging over the wall.

She said, 'There's nothing here to scare me.' She felt a little chilly. 'There's nothing here to touch me. Grandmother will be so happy.'

And she broke two branches of the holly. She made a lovely little bunch. 'Oh Granny will love this,' she said. 'This will be a present for Grandmother.'

And then she made her way down the wall. But then she stood on a stone that was loose and she slipped and fell. She rolled and tumbled. She held on to the holly as she tumbled down, and hit her knee on a big sharp stone. She was dazed. Then she lay there and looked at her knee. It was a great gash on her knee, split all the way down.

And she said, 'Oh Granny'll be so upset! Whatever shall I do?' The blood began to run down over her little sock. 'What shall I do? Granny will be so angry with me now, so angry! And I promised her faithfully I wouldn't come near this place.'

Jenny was still hanging on to the holly. Now before her was a large wall. She was rather dazed. And as she looked she saw a little door in the wall. She said to herself, 'Granny never said there was a door in the wall.'

And then the door opened with a scree-ee-e-e-k. Jenny was amazed. She saw a little tiny face peeping through the wall.

She said, 'Granny was right! There's something strange about this place. And I cannot walk, my knee is so sore!'

Then the little tiny face came out and she saw that it had long, grey hair hanging down. The nose was long and pointed. She could see the face of an old woman.

'Oh!' Jenny says. 'It's the ghost, the ghost of the castle. She's going to take me away.'

And she's still hanging on to her little bunch of holly. The little door opened wider with a scree-eek. And the old woman came out. And Jenny could see that she had a long, dark dress trailing to her feet.

She came up and said in a shaky voice, 'Don't be afraid, little one. No one's going to hurt you.'

But Jenny stood terrified, she couldn't move. The old woman came closer and closer and Jenny said, 'Keep away from me, old woman! You're the ghost of the castle and Granny's warned me. I should never have come here.'

'Don't be afraid, little one, I'm not going to hurt you.' And the old woman stood before her. Then Jenny smelled a strange musky smell, a cold, damp smell. She said, 'Let me mend your leg for you. I see you have hurt yourself.'

And she reached over and caught Jenny by the hand. Jenny saw that her fingers were curled; the nails were brown and grey. And the old woman's hands Jenny felt were cold as clay.

'Rise up, little one,' she says, 'come with me! I will fix you – you have nothing to fear.'

Jenny struggled up and the old woman pulled her gradually. She took her through the little door in the wall. There was a little room. And the old woman closed the door behind her.

Jenny smelled this strange musky smell of cold and damp. She looked and stared. There were coffins all around the wall! And on the stone shelves were skulls sitting, staring. Jenny was terrified.

'Please, old woman,' she said, 'I-let me go! Let me out of here. This is terrible.'

The old woman said, 'Don't be afraid! These are my family. You have a family, haven't you?'

'No, I live with my Grandmother. And she's warned me not to come here.'

She says, 'No one's going to hurt you! Just you come over here.' There was a stone chair. The old woman said, 'Sit you down there!'

And Jenny sat down, trembling with fear. The blood was running from a large gash in her knee, running over her little sock.

The old woman said, 'Don't be afraid. These are my people. I am the guardian of my people.'

And the coffins were piled deep round the whole wall. Some were twisted, and Jenny could see bones sticking out from some of the coffins. All these heads were placed on stone slabs around the wall. Jenny was terrified and thought she saw the eyes watching her, the empty eyeholes.

And the old woman said again, 'My dear, you have nothing to fear. I will fix your leg for you.'

Then she took an old cloth and with a piece of it she cleaned the blood away from the large gash on Jenny's knee. She wrapped the rest of the cloth around Jenny's leg as the blood ran over her stocking.

The old woman said, 'Now that looks really well, my dear.'

And Jenny saw these big curled fingers, the little face and the long grey hair. But the old woman's eyes were kindly. Jenny was still hanging on to her little bunch of holly.

She said, 'I see you've taken something from my favourite tree – that is the tree of my father. Now, my dear, you must go home to your grandmother.'

And she led her through the little door. Jenny limped through terrified. And the little door closed with a scree-ee-k.

Jenny turned round ... it was gone. Only the bare wall! And she looked at her leg. She saw the bandage, and she saw that she still had the holly in her hand. Her leg felt a little better.

'Oh,' she said, 'whatever shall I tell my grandmother when I get home?' So she walked home and her grand-mother was waiting for her.

She says, 'Jenny, where have you been? You've been gone a long time. School was out a while ago.'

'Oh Grandmother,' she said, 'I am sorry, so sorry. I wanted to find a present for you and I climbed the castle wall to get some holly for you. And I fell. I gashed my leg.'

The old granny looked and saw there was a bandage around her leg. She said, 'My dear, come in!' And she brought little Jenny into the little kitchen of the house where they lived. 'Sit you down there. Granny's not going to argue with you. What happened to you?'

'Oh Grandmother,' she said, 'I climbed the castle wall to get you a little holly. And then I fell and I slipped. A little door opened in the wall. And an old lady brought me in. Granny, it was horrible! Terrible – all those coffins and all those skulls that were staring at me, Grandmother. And that old woman. She looked horrible, but she was so nice.'

'Whatever happened to you, my dear? Why have you got a bandage around your leg?'

'Oh Grandmother, my leg is gashed. It's a terrible cut.' And the blood had dried on her little sock.

Grandmother said, 'Let me have a look.' And very carefully she wound the cloth off little Jenny's leg. As she unwound the cloth it just melted in her hands, fell down piece by piece on the floor. She said, 'Jenny, wherever did you get that piece of cloth?'

'I told you, Granny, it was the old woman!'

And Granny looked: 'Jenny, there's no gash on your leg, my dear—' and she pulled the last bit of cloth away. There was a scar, but no cut on Jenny's leg. She said, 'Jenny, you are a very lucky girl.'

'But Grandmother, she never hurt me. She was just kind to me, really kind. But the room was so cold.'

'Jenny,' she said, 'my dear, didn't I warn you a long time ago not to go to the castle?'

'But I had to go, Granny. I wanted to get you a present for Christmas.'

And Granny picked up the little bunch of holly. 'Jenny, you've brought me the greatest present of all for my Christmas – you've brought me back your self!'

And Jenny lived with her granny for many, many years and she never was afraid anymore as she walked by that castle to school. Because she knew she had met the guardian of the castle, who guarded the family of all those people who were gone a long time before her.

And that is the end of my story.

# Johnny MacDonald
# and the Three Skeletons

Now many stories were laid towards many people's door-ways that never actually happened to them, but in folklore they had to find a character like Homer, like King Arthur, to lay some of these good stories towards. And among Traveller lore we have the same idea; we have a famous character called John MacDonald. And John MacDonald was a piper, there are even tunes called after him. And he was a good storyteller in his time, he was a good piper forbyes – whether he made stories up or not. But one I'd like to tell you this morning is about John MacDonald.

John MacDonald was a Travelling man, he was a wandering piper, a good piper. And he had a wife and two little boys. He never owned a horse in his life. He had no time for horses. But he had a little homemade handcart he built himself. And he and his wife would wander the country-side. He would play his pipes at the guest houses. He was always welcome wherever he would be.

But when he got together with the Traveller community, when some Travellers met together on a campsite way back in time, the most interesting character was a bit like myself; John MacDonald was a storyteller. And to get round John Mac-Donald's fire was a treat! And listen to some of his stories. This is one that was supposed to happen to him. So, just you listen!

One day John and his wife had been travelling all day long. They didn't have any girls, just two little boys, and they walked by their daddy's side. And his wife Mary, she would hawk the doors along. He would make baskets for her, he would make scrubbers and besoms and he would pipe in his own time. But it was a late evening, the fall of the year, about October, and they came to a local camping site by the roadway, which was well used by Travelling folk.

And Travelling people in those days, the original Travellers, always cleaned up. The only thing they never cleaned up – they burned up all the sticks that was left – they never left a bit of stick. They left the stones in a little heap, for people would put them on their canvas to keep the canvas down. But they would never leave any firewood. They would make sure all the firewood was burned up.

So John and his wife Mary, they pulled into the little camping site. And the two little boys were tired, they sat down. He took off the campsticks they carried with them, always tied along his little handcart. And his Mary was clever, she was a real Traveller woman.

He says, 'Mary, you put up the tent there in two minutes. And I'll go and see if I can get some sticks to make a cup of tea for the weans!'

Now he looked up; there's wall, a high wall, and he could see the tops of holly trees. But the tops of the holly trees were rotten.

And he says, 'I'll just climb that wall, stand on the wall and I'll break some of the tops of thon sticks and we'll have a fire in nae time.'

So Mary got the camp sticks, she was busy putting up the tent. And John climbed up the wall, which was about six foot high; he was a supple man. And he stood on the top of the wall. He was level with the rotten tops of the holly that went round the wall. And he's breaking them off, and he broke this big chunk of rotten stick, when he looked at the graveyard and it started – REETLE RATTLE REETLE RATTLE REETLE RATTLE – in the graveyard.

And he stared in amazement, for here were three skeletons, two big ones and a smaller one. The two big ones were laying into the little one. And they were beating and battering and kicking him and punching him.

'Upon my soul,' said John MacDonald, he says, 'two to one is not my kind of thing.'

And he jumps down into the graveyard with a piece of stick in his hand. Within minutes he took the little one's part and he scattered the bones of the two big ones. He scattered their skulls, and he scattered the bones. He says, 'Two to one is no my kind of thing!'

And the little one stood by and watched this. And then an amazing thing happened. Lo and behold he began to change . . . he turned into a young farmer dressed in tweeds.

And he said, 'Thank you! Now I can rest in peace.'

John MacDonald was amazed. He said 'A-a-ar-are you a ghost?'

'Well,' he said, 'you could say I'm a ghost.' He said, 'These were . . .' but then the skeletons vanished, the remains of the skeletons vanished! When he took human form they vanished. 'These,' he said, 'were my two brothers. And they killed me for my father's money. And I could never rest in peace. But you,' he said, 'came to my part. If you had hae been there when they were beating me up to kill me, it would never have happened. And you have been honest and true! And for that I'm going to give my money to you, because they never got it. Both were hanged with my murder.'

Now he said, 'Tonight when it gets dark I want you to backtrack the way you came today. And you'll see a large pine tree in a farm road-end. Follow that road-end up till you come to another pine tree, and by the side of that pine tree you'll see a well, a dry well. Go down the dry well – it's easy access – and there at the very bottom stone pull it out. See what you find.' And the skeleton faded away, and was gone.

John MacDonald was amazed, he didn't know what to do. Never mentioned it to his wife. But he came over with some sticks, and they kindled a fire, they had a cup of tea.

She asked him, something to eat; 'No,' he says, 'I'm no needing something to eat.' He was so excited he didna ken what was wrong with him. He never mentioned it to his wife.

So that night when it got gloaming dark, he says, 'Mary, I have to go back the road a wee bit.'

She says, 'What are you going back for? I'm eerie to sit here by myself.' (Eerie means 'feart' or afraid.)

He said, 'I'll no be long.'

She said, 'What is it you're going for?'

'Well,' he said, 'I saw a field of potatoes, a pit of potatoes away back the road, I'm going to go back and get a few tatties for the weans, for the morning.'

'Well,' she says, 'dinna be long!'

'Well,' he said, 'sit in the tent where nobody'll see you.'

So Mary took the wee weans, the two wee laddies, inside the tent and she began to tell them a story. She just lighted a candle and she begint to tell the weans a story.

And he made his way back till he came to the big pine tree. He saw an old rough farm road and he followed it up for a little way. He saw another pine tree and some buildings. And as the ghost had told him, he went over and there was an old, dry, draw-well with a lid.

He pulled the lid off and he climbed down. The well was dry. He pulled out the watering stone as the skeleton had said, and he pulled out a wee little iron box. It was full of gold sovereigns, packed full of gold sovereigns! More money than he'd ever seen in his life.

Of course he carried it back with him to his tent and he told Mary the story, with the two wee laddies sitting playing with the gold sovereigns. So he didn't know what to do.

He said, 'We'll no shift today.'

So he went and dug a hole and buried the box. And tied all the gold sovereigns into a pack with Mary's shawl.

And the next day he went down to the village. He says, 'Mary, I'm sick fed up travelling!' He bought himself a wee house, sent the two laddies to school.

Nobody ever knew where John MacDonald's money came from. And it was on his dying bed that he told some of his family where he actually got the money.

And that was the story of Johnny MacDonald.

And there were many, many wonderful stories laid at Johnny's door; he was a kind of a Donald Angie MacDougal MacLean in Traveller folklore.

# Jack and the Devil's Purse

A long time ago in the West Highlands of Scotland Jack lived with his old mother on a little croft. His father had died when he was very young and Jack barely remembered him. He spent most of his time with his mother. They had a few goats and a couple of sheep on their small croft. His mother kept a few hens and she sold a few eggs in the village. She took in washing and knitting and doing everything else just to keep her and her son alive. But Jack grew up. He loved and respected his mother. And he tried to make the croft work, but things got very hard. The ground was too hard and stony, little crops could he grow. He always depended on the few shillings that his mother could bring in because he couldn't get very much off the land. And where they stayed was about two miles from the small village. There was a post office and a local store and a little inn. Jack used to walk there every week to get his mother's few groceries, or messages. And Jack had grown up to be a young man by this time.

So one day his mother called him, 'Jack, are you busy?'

'Well no, Mother, I'm no busy. I've cut the wee puckle hay and I've stacked it up, it's no much.'

'Would you like to go into the village and get something for me?'

'Of course, Mother, I always go, you know I always go.'

So she gave him a few shillings to walk into the village. And he went into the store and bought these few groceries for his mother. He came walking across the little street, and lo and behold he was stopped by an old friend of his mother's who had never seen her for many years. But the friend knew him.

'Oh, Jack,' he said, 'you're finally grown up to a big, handsome young man.'

Jack said, 'Do I know you, sir?'

'Och laddie,' he said, 'ye ken ye know me: I'm a friend o' yer mother's.'

'Well,' Jack said, 'I've never remembered much about you.'

'Oh, but your mother does! Tell her old Dougald was askin for her when ye go back. I was your mother's lover, you know.'

'Oh well, that's nothin to do with me.'

'Well, tell your mother I'll come out and see her first chance I get,' he said. 'I've been away travelling. But now I'm back and I'm settled here in the village. I'll prob'ly come out and see her sometime.'

'Okay,' says Jack, 'I'll have to hurry.

'Oh no, laddie, ye're no goin awa like that! Come in wi me!'

'Where?'

He says, 'Into the inn.'

Jack says, 'The inn? Sir, I don't—'

'Dinna call me sir,' he said, 'call me Dougald!'

'Sir, I never was in an inn in my life.'

'Oh laddie, you mean to tell me you've never had a drink?'

'No me, Dougald, I've never had a drink.'

'Well, you're gettin one now! Come wi me.'

Into the little inn. Jack had his mother's little groceries. He placed them beside the bar.

'Two glasses of whisky!' Full glasses of whisky . . . 'Right,' said old Dougald, who'd had a few glasses before that, 'drink it up, laddie! It's good for ye. And I'm comin to see yer mother, mind and tell her!'

Jack drank the glass o' whisky for the first time in his life. Oh, he choked and coughed a little bit and it felt strange to him. He had never had a drink before in his life. But after a few seconds when the warm glow began to pass across his chest and his head began to get a little dizzy, Jack felt good!

And old Dougald said, 'Did you like that?'

Jack said, 'Of course, it was good.'

'Have another one!' So he filled another glass for Jack and Jack had two full glasses of whisky for the first time in his life.

He said, 'Well now,' he was feeling a wee bit tipsy; 'I think I'd better go home wi my mother's groceries!'

'Okay, laddie, mind my message now! Tell yer mother I'll come out to see her because she's an old girlfriend o' mine!' Old Dougald was well on with drink.

Jack picked up his little bag and he walked back . . . two steps forward, three steps back. But he made his way to his mother.

When he walked in his mother was pleased to see him. She said, 'Your supper's on the table.'

'I'm no wantin any supper, Mother.'

She said, 'Jack, have you been drinkin? You know, Jack, drink ruined yer father. It was drink that killed yer father.'

'Oh, Mother, I had the best fun o' my life. In fact I met an old boyfriend o' yours!'

And she touched her hair and pulled her apron down, you know. She smoothed her apron. She said, 'What did you say, laddie?'

'Mother, I met an old boyfriend o' yours!'

And she tidied her hair, pulled down her apron and said, 'What did you say?'

'I met an old boyfriend o' yours and he's comin to see ye!'

'A . . . my boyfriend? I have nae boyfriends, laddie.'

'Aye, Mother, you've had a boyfriend – before you met my father.'

'What's his name?'

'Dougald.

'Oh,' she said, 'young Dougald, young Dougald! God, laddie, I've never seen him for years.'

'Well, Mother, he's comin to see you onyway.'

She was pleased about this. She'd forgot about Jack's drinking. So they sat and they talked and they discussed things. And things went on as usual.

But Jack had the taste of drink. Now every time he went to the village he would say: 'Mother, could I borrow a shilling fae ye,' or two shillings or three shillings, every time for the sake o' getting a drink. Till there was no money left, there was no money coming into the croft by his work or his mother had nothing to spare. She gave him what she could afford to buy the messages and that was all.

'Mother,' he said, 'gie us a shilling or something!'

'No, son, I havena got it.'

'Anyway,' he says, 'I'll walk to the village.'

So on the road to the village there was a crossroads: one road went to the left, one road went to the right. Jack was coming walking down.

He said, 'God upon my soul, bless my body in Hell, and Devil . . .' he's cursing to himself. 'What would I give for a shilling! My mother has nae money. She's gien me everything she had. God, I could do with a drink. I could do, I could walk in an' buy myself a glass o' whisky and really enjoy it. God Almighty, what's wrong with me?'

No answer.

He said, 'The Devil o' Hell – will ye listen to me? I'd give my soul tonight to the Devil o' Hell if he would only give me a shilling for a drink!'

But lo and behold Jack walked on and there at the cross-roads stood a tall, dark man. Jack was about to pass him by when, 'Aye, Jack,' he said, 'you're makin your way to the village.'

Jack looked up. He said, 'Sir, do you know me?'

'Ah, Jack, I ken you all right. You and your mother are up in that croft there.'

But Jack said, 'I've never met you, sir.'

'No, Jack,' said the man, 'you've never met me. But I heard you muttering to yourself as you were comin down the road. And the things you were sayin I was interested in.'

Jack said, 'What do you think I was sayin?'

'Oh, ye talked about your God . . . and you mentioned my name.'

'*Your* name?'

'Of course, you mentioned my name, Jack – I'm the Devil.'

'You're the Devil?' says Jack.

'I am the Devil, Jack,' he said. 'And you said you would gie me your soul for a shilling for a drink.'

Jack said, 'Look, let you be the Devil of Hell or the Devil of Nowhere, I would give my soul to the Devil, the *real* Devil tonight!'

He says, 'Jack, I am *the real Devil!*'

'Ah,' Jack says, 'I dinna believe ye.'

'Well,' he said, 'can you try me?'

Jack said, 'What do I try ye for? What hae ye got to gie me? Hae you got a shilling for me?'

The Devil says, 'I'll go one better.' Puts his hand under his cloak and he brings out a small leather purse. 'Jack, look, you said you would sell your soul to the Devil for a shilling for a drink.'

Jack says, 'Gladly I would.'

'Well,' the Devil says, 'look . . . I've got a purse here and in that purse is a shilling. But I'll go one better – every time you take a shilling out, another one'll take its place – and you can drink to your heart's content. You'll never need to worry again. But on one condition.'

'And what's your condition?' says Jack.

He said, 'You said you would give me your soul!'

Jack said, 'If you're the Devil you can have my soul – it's no good to me. A drink I need!'

'Take my purse,' said the Devil, 'and spend to your heart's content, and I'll come for you in a year and a day.'

'Done,' says Jack, 'show me your purse!'

The Devil gave Jack the little purse. And he opened it up. A silver shilling lay in the purse.

'Right,' says Jack, 'it's a deal!'

The Devil was gone, he vanished.

Jack walked to the village, spent his mother's two-three shillings to buy the things his mother needed. And he said: 'I've got a shilling in my purse.'

He walked across to the local inn. Took the shilling out, put it on the bar and called for a glass of whisky. Got his glass of whisky, drank it up. Called for another one and drank it up. 'Now,' he said, 'Devil, if you're telling the truth . . .' And he opened the purse. Lo and behold, there was another shilling! He spent another one and another one took its place. Jack got really drunk. He walked home to his mother, purse in his hip pocket.

'Now at last,' he said, 'I can drink to my heart's content.' He gave his mother her messages.

'Where did you get the money to drink, Jack?' she says. 'You've been drinkin.'

'Och, I met a couple o' friends, Mother.' (He never told her.)

But anyhow, Jack made every excuse he could get to go to the village. And every time he went he got drunk, as usual. Day out and day in. Oh, he bought things for his mother forbyes.

But one night after three months had passed she said, 'Jack, you've been drinkin a terrible lot. Where are you gettin all this money?'

'Ach, Mother, it's only friends I meet.' But she was pleased with that.

But after six months, after Jack had been drinking for another three months, she said, 'Jack, look, you'll have to tell me the truth: where is this money coming from? You've been drunk now for weeks on end. Not that I'm complainin . . . drink killed your father. It'll prob'ly kill you too. You're a young man and it's none o' my business.'

'Ach, Mother, it's only money I've been gettin from my friends. They owed it to me.'

Another three months passed and nine months had passed. Jack was still drinking to his heart's content. One night he came home very drunk.

She says, 'Jack, do you know what you're doin? That's nine month you've been drinkin every week. Laddie, ye ken you're workin with the Devil!'

He says, 'What, Mother?'

'Laddie, you're workin with the Devil. Drink is Devil's work. It killed yer father and it'll kill you.'

'But, Mother, what do you mean?'

'Well, I'm telling you, laddie, *it's Devil's work!* Laddie, where are ye gettin the money?'

'Well, Mother, to tell ye the truth, I really met the Devil.'

'Ye met the Devil?' says his mother.

'Aye, Mother, I met the Devil. And he's comin for me – in a year's time.'

'But,' she said, 'what do ye mean?'

'Well, to tell you the truth: I coaxed you for a shilling and I begged you for money. I was cursin and swearin at the crossroads and there I met a man. And he gave me a purse wi a shilling in it. And I sold my soul to him. He tellt me he's comin for me in a year and a day.'

She said, 'Laddie, where is the purse?'

Jack took the purse from his pocket and the old woman looked. It was a queer looking purse. She had never seen nothing like this before.

He said, 'Look in it, Mother, see what's in it.'

And the mother looked in. There was a single shilling in it, a silver shilling.

He said, 'Mother, tak it out.'

And the old mother took it out. She held it in her hand.

'Now,' he said, 'look in there, Mother!'

And she looked again: there was another one. She took another, and another one took its place. Oh, she catcht it and clashed it to the floor.

She says, 'Laddie, that's *the Devil's purse* you've got!'

'But,' he says, 'Mother, what can I do with it?'

She says, 'Laddie, get rid of it. Ye ken the Devil's got ye!'

'But,' he says, 'Mother, I've tried. I'm beginning to understand now that your words are true. I threw it in the fire when you werena lookin, but it jumped back out again. I throw it away, it comes back in my pocket again. Mother, what am I goin to do? I dinna want to go wi' the Devil!'

Now Jack began to get to his senses. He stopped drinking for a week, never had a drink. One shilling lay in the purse.

He said, 'Mother, what can I do? He's comin for me!'

'Oh I ken, laddie, he's comin for ye. We ken that. You shouldna hae took it from him in the first place.'

'Mother,' he says, 'help me, please! I dinna want to go wi the Devil!'

'Well,' she says, 'look, Jack, there's only one thing I can tell ye: I have an old sister you've never met, your auntie, and she lives a long way from here, Jack. I was always askin ye to go and see her for a visit. She's an old henwife and people thinks that she's a bit of a witch, and if onybody can help you, she's the only one that can. Would you tak my word, Jack, forget about the purse! Tak it wi ye, show it to her and explain yer case to her.'

'But where does she bide, Mother? Ye never tellt me this afore.'

'Oh, laddie,' she said, 'it's a long way fae here.'

'Well,' he said, 'Mother, if she can help me I'm goin to see her!'

So the old woman told Jack where her old sister stayed. And the next morning Jack went on his way to find his old auntie. He travelled on for days and days and he finally came to his old auntie's little cottage. She had a cottage on the beach by the shoreside and she kept hens and ducks. He walked up and knocked at the door.

And a very old bended woman came out and said: 'Hello, young man! What do you want here?'

He said, 'Auntie, do ye no ken who I am?'

She says, 'What do ye mean? I'm no auntie of yours!'

He says, 'I'm Jack, I'm your sister's on.'

'Oh,' she said, 'my sister's son from the farthest point of Ireland! I never, never thought you would ever come and see me. Come in, laddie, come in! I'm pleased to see ye. And how's my old sister?'

'Yer old sister's fine,' he said. 'But it's me I'm worried about.'

'And what's wrong wi you, laddie?' she said, after he'd had a wee bite to eat.

'Well look, Auntie, to tell ye the God's truth: I'm tooken over wi the Devil.'

'Oh dear me, laddie,' she says, 'sit down and tell me about it.'

So Jack told her the story I'm telling you.

She says, 'Laddie, show me the purse!'

And she took the purse, she opened it. There was one single shilling in it. She took the shilling out and she looked again – another one took its place. She took the first shilling, put it back in and the other one vanished.

She said, 'Laddie, you're really tooken over wi the Devil; that's the God's truth!' So she took the purse and she put it on the little table. She said, 'Jack, there's only one thing ye can do. But wait a minute . . . ye can stay here the night with me. But tomorrow morning you want to go up to the village and see the local blacksmith. Tell him to put the purse on the anvil in the smiddie and to heat a horseshoe in the fire and beat that purse like he's never beat anything before in his life! But I have a wee present for ye and I'll gie it to you in the mornin.'

So Jack spent a restless night with his old auntie. But next morning after breakfast she came out. She had a wee small Bible that you could barely see, the smallest Bible you could ever see!

She said, 'Jack, put *that* in your pocket and don't part wi it for nobody under the sun!'

So Jack took the wee Bible and he put it in his pocket. He thanked his old auntie very much and told her he would go to the blacksmith and see him.

'Tell him I sent ye! Tell him old Isa sent ye up!'

So Jack bade farewell to his auntie, walked up to the little village and came to the blacksmith's shop. The old blacksmith was busy over the fire with a bit leather apron round his waist. There wasn't a horse in the smiddie or nothing. And Jack walked in. The old blacksmith was blowin up the fire.

He turned round, said, 'Hello, young man! What can I do for ye? Ye got a horse with ye?'

'No,' Jack said, 'I've no horse, sir. I've no horse. I was down talking to my auntie, old Isa.'

'Oh, old Isa!' said the blacksmith, 'oh, the old friend o' mine. Aye, what can I do for ye?'

'Well,' he says, 'I'm her nephew. And I want you to help me.'

'Oh,' he says, 'any friend of old Isa's is a friend o' mine. What can I do for ye?'

'Well,' he says, 'sir, look, it's this purse. It belongs to the Devil!'

'Oh, belongs to the Devil,' said the blacksmith, 'I see. And what am I supposed to do with it? Throw it in the fire?'

'Oh no,' Jack said, 'you'll no throw it in the fire; I want ye to put it on the anvil and beat it! My auntie says to beat it with a horseshoe.'

'Well, your auntie cured me many times when I was sick. And what *she* says is bound to be true.'

So the old blacksmith took the purse and he put it on the anvil. And he went in, got a big horseshoe; he put it on a pair o' clippers and held it in the fire. And he held it till the shoe was red-hot. He took and he beat the purse. And every time he beat the purse a little imp jumped out! It stood on the floor, ugly little creature with its long nails and ugly-looking face. And the blacksmith beat the purse . . . another one and another one and another one came out. Till there were about fifteen or sixteen imps – all standing there looking up with their curled nails and their ugly little faces, eyes upside-down and ears twisted. They were the ugliest looking things you ever saw! The blacksmith and Jack paid no attention to them. And then the last beat – out jumped Himself, the Devil! And within minutes he was tall and dark.

He turns round to the blacksmith and to Jack: 'Aye, Jack,' he says, 'heh-h, laddie, ye thought you could beat me, didn't ye? You thought you could beat me by beatin this purse! But laddie, that maks nae difference, you only beat the imps out, and they're mine. And *you're* still belongin to me!'

The old blacksmith stood in a shake. He was terrified. He said, 'I–I had nothing to do with it.'

Devil said, 'Look, nothing to do with you, old man, nothing to do with you. Tend to your fire. This young man is my problem.' He said, 'Jack, you thought you could beat me, didn't ye? I've come for you, Jack, you've got to come wi me!' And all the little imps are gathered round in a knot together and they are standing there, they're watching and they're hanging on to the Devil's legs. He says, 'Jack, you've got to come with me!'

But Jack says, 'I'm no dead yet.'

He says, 'That was no bargain – I never mentioned you being dead. You told me you'd sell me your soul, so you must come with me!'

'Well,' Jack says, 'if that's it, that's it!'

So the Devil walked out from the blacksmith's shop with the imps all behind him. And he and Jack went on their way. They travelled for days and weeks through thorns and brambles and forests and places, caverns and valleys, till at last they came into Hell. And there in Hell was a great cavern with a great roaring fire, and all these little cages full of imps. The Devil opened an empty one and he put all the little ones in, hushed them in and he closed the door.

They stood with their nails against the cages, their ugly faces – some with faces of old women, some with faces of old men, ears upside-down – the most ugly-looking creatures you ever saw in your lifetime.

'Now,' says the Devil, 'I've got you!'

'Well,' Jack says, 'what are you goin to do with me?'

'Well, Jack,' he said, 'to tell ye the truth, I don't know what I'm goin to do with you. You spent my money, ye know, and you enjoyed yourself.'

'That's true,' said Jack, 'I enjoyed myself.'

'And you tried to deceive me.'

'That's right,' said Jack, 'I did try.'

'But,' he says, 'I finally got ye. But I'll be lenient with you, Jack, if you'll do something for me!'

Jack said, 'Well?'

He said, 'I'm goin away for a long time, Jack. I must go on a journey. I have some people to see in a faraway country who are due a visit from me, the Devil! And all I want you to do is to sit here by the fire and take care of the imps while I'm gone.'

'Oh,' Jack said, 'that's no problem, no problem at all.'

So then there was a flash of light and the Devil was gone. Jack was left all alone in Hell. Cages and cages all around him, a burning fire . . . all by himself.

So he sat for many hours wearied and wondering, how in the world was he going to get away back from Hell? Thinking about himself, thinking about everything else and then lo and behold! He put his hand in his pocket and he felt the little Bible that his auntie had given him. He brought it forward. He looked at it and he opened the first page. And because he had nobody to talk to and the light was so bright by the fireside, and he was wearied, he thought to himself he would read – though he'd never read the Bible before in his life.

He turned the pages and he got kind of interested. And he sat there reading and reading and reading . . . quiet and still it was in Hell. He looked all around. All the little imps were up with their nails against the cages, and they were peaceful and quiet. They were not doing anything. Jack was reading away to himself.

And then he said to them, 'Would ye like a story?'

They did not say a word.

So Jack started and he read aloud from the Bible. All the imps gathered round their cages with their hands round the steel bars, and they were sitting listening, so intent. Jack read page after page from the Bible and they were so interested. Then Jack stopped.

And the moment he stopped they started the wildest carry-on! They were screaming, they were fighting and arguing with each other and biting each other, aargh! Jack opened the Bible again and then the screaming stopped.

'Aha,' said Jack, 'it's stories ye like, isn't it?'

He went round every cage in Hell and opened them all. He let them all out. They gathered round him by the fireside. They sat on his legs, they climbed on his knees. They keeked into his ears, they sat on his head, they pulled on his ears and pulled his hair. And then Jack started reading aloud from the Bible. They sat quietly listening. And he read the Bible through and through and through for many, many times. He must have read the Bible through a dozen times, and they enjoyed it. But the moment he stopped, they started arguing again and fighting! So to keep them quiet Jack kept reading the Bible. And the more he read the quieter they were.

'So,' Jack said, 'the only way that I'm going to get peace is to read the Bible to you!' So he read the Bible through a hundred times.

And then there was a flash of light! There stood the Devil with an old man on his back. He came up and threw the old man in the fire.

'Right, imps,' he said, 'come on and get your spears, get this old man tortured!'

But they all ran behind Jack. They curled behind his legs, they climbed behind his back. And they wouldn't look at the Devil.

'Come on, imps,' said the Devil, 'there's work to be done!'

But the imps wouldn't look at the Devil in any way, they paid him no attention.

The Devil said, 'Jack, what have you done to my imps?'

Jack said, 'I've done nothing to them. I read them a story.'

'A story!' says the Devil. 'Where did you read them a story?'

'From the Bible.'

'Take *that* from me,' said the Devil, 'take *that* from me, put *that* away from me!' He says, 'Jack, you're no good to me. No good to me, I'm sorry I ever even thought about you in the first place. Jack, you're too bad for Heaven and you're too good for Hell. Look, I'm goin to give you a chance. You take all these imps and go and start a place for yourself! I'll set you free. Now be on your way! And *that*'s the road to take—' there was a space o' light.

And Jack walked on. 'Goodbye, Devil,' he said, and he walked on through the space o' light and travelled on.

Lo and behold all the little imps, one after the other, followed him in a single file till he disappeared from the cavern o' Hell. When the beautiful sun was shining he landed in a beautiful forest. And he sat down there. He wondered: 'Am I really free from Hell?' he said. 'Will the Devil ever bother me anymore?'

And all the little imps gathered round him. They sat on his knees, they sat beside him.

And Jack said, 'Well little fellas, we have a problem. You know I've led you from Hell. Now I canna take you back to my mother in any way. But look, this is a nice place for you to live. Go out in the forest and be good and kind and create in your own likeness, and enjoy yourselves. Make a home for yourselves here. You'll never need to go back to Hell again!'

And then the little fellas vanished in the forest.

Jack walked on to his mother's. And his mother was pleased to see him.

'Did ye do what I told you, Jack?' she said.

'Aye, Mother, I did what you tellt me, and have I got a story to tell you!'

So the little imps lived in the forest and they spread out. They created in their likeness. And therefore began the legend of all the goblins and elves and gnomes in the land. And Jack lived happy with his mother. But he never took another drink.

And that is the end of my story!

# Two Ravens

Jack stayed with his mother in this little cottage many, many years ago, long before your day and mine. And all they had was a vegetable patch. Jack used to grow vegetables of all description. He was a good gardener, and he had a few hens. He and his mother managed to survive by selling a few eggs and vegetables in the village. Whatever Jack sold the vegetables for he would always use to bring back some messages. And he always managed to bring his mother back a shilling or two, which she promised she would save for Jack for when she was gone. Maybe it was only a shilling, maybe two, but he always gave her the change that was left. Jack was not a drinker, no way. But he had one vice – every spare moment he had he spent it . . . fishing.

Now, past Jack's place where he stayed ran a large river, and it travelled into the hills for hundreds of miles. One morning he packed his basket with the vegetables, went into the market and sold them. He hurried the best he could because he wanted to fish. He got some things for his mother, hurried back and swallowed a quick meal.

She says, 'Jack, you're in an awful hurry.'

'Well, Mother, you know,' he said, 'there was rain last night and the burn's big.'

'I trust between you and the burn, laddie,' she said, 'something bad's going to happen to you, with all this carry-on fishing! You never, never give a thought to anything else as long as you can get out there with that rod and sit fishing!'

He says, 'Mother, don't I bring you back some good fish sometimes?'

She says, 'Sometimes you do well, Jack. But do you give a thought to me – I might want you to sit and talk to me – and do you give a thought to other things to do past your own sport?'

He says, 'Mother, look, you know where I am when I'm going fishing!'

But she says, 'Jack, I know you go fishing, but you're away for so long; you spend hours at a time and that burn goes for miles. You could fall into the burn, get drowned or something, I would never ken.'

'Mother, you reared me up, now I'm eighteen years of age,' he says. 'Have I ever in the world ever gien ye any worry or grievances over me?'

She said, 'You give me plenty worry when you go fishing, Jack!'

'Well,' he says, 'I'm going fishing today. And I'm thinking to travel a wee bit further up the burn. That burn goes for hundreds of miles and I've never been up very far. I'm going to walk a long way till I get to the place I've never fished before, and fish it!'

She says, 'Jack, you're going to the Land of the Ravens!'

'Tsst, Ravens, Mother!' he said, 'you and your fairy tales.'

'If you go too far up the burn you'll go to the Land of the Ravens,' she said, 'and you ken what'll happen to you if *they* come across you!'

'Mother, I'm no worried about Ravens,' he said, 'that's only fairy stories, folklore. There nae such thing as Ravens!'

She said, 'If the Ravens get you fishing in their land, Jack, I'm telling you, you'll never get back!'

'Anyway, we're no going to argue about it,' Jack says.

He went into the garden, got a spade and dug a large tin of worms, packed his bag, got his fishing rod, collected all his hooks and bits of line – all that he could in case he would lose them in the burn – put them in his bag and flung it on his back, bade goodbye to his mother. And away he goes.

He walked and he walked up the burn past the places he used to fish fill he came to a part where he'd never fished. And he started, put the worms on his hook and fished. Oh, and he was getting good trout, you know, putting them in his bag. The wee ones he was flinging back. And he walked on and on till he came to a cliff face. The burn was dropping into a large waterfall.

'Now,' Jack said, 'the burn will be a large pool down there beside that waterfall. If I could make my way to it I bet ye I could sit there all day and get plenty! In that big pool there's bound to be plenty fish. I've never been here before.' So he stepped through the wood, said, 'If I can go round about it and go down through the trees I might find a pathway to the foot of the falls.'

And so he did. He found a well-worn path like a deer track and followed it right down a steep bank. He looked up when he saw this great big waterfall! It was shooting over the face of the cliff, falling into this great big pool, oh, maybe a hundred yards in diameter.

He said, 'This is the place for me!' And there were large stones around the foot of the fall.

Jack walked down. When he came to the foot of the pool he came round behind the boulders and looked – sitting on the rock beside the pool was the bonniest young woman Jack had ever seen in his life! Jack was amazed. And he was staring at the young woman. But the thing that mesmerised Jack most of all – sitting beside her on the same rock was the largest eagle Jack had ever seen in his life – with beady eyes and great big curled claws. It was watching Jack. Jack didn't know whether to go forward or back. And he had the fishing rod in his hand. He walked down.

The young woman spoke to him, 'Good morning, young man!'

Jack kind of hesitated, you know, and he's watching this eagle: 'Good morning! Good morning,' he said.

She says, 'Have you been fishing?'

'Yes,' he said, 'I've been fishing.'

She said, 'Had ye any luck? Did you catch many?'

And Jack looked. She was dressed in skin from head to foot. She had the most beautiful flaxen fair hair hanging down her back. Jack eyed her up from head to foot. But the thing he looked at most of all was her boots. She had the most beautiful pair of boots on that Jack had ever seen in his life, made of the finest leather and carved with all the animals of the forest.

So the young lady says, 'Young man, don't be afraid. Just carry on, go on with your fishing!'

But Jack didn't start fishing.

'My lady,' he said, 'I've never come here before to fish. This is as far as I've ever come. I'm amazed to see another person here before me. Do you do any fishing?'

'No,' she said, 'I don't do fishing. We come here for solitude, me and Hungry.'

He said, 'You and who?'

She said, 'Me and Hungry, my eagle.'

Jack looked at this bird, and this bird was eyeing him up. Its eyes were so bright and staring. Jack was a wee bit wary, you know.

She said, 'And he's always hungry. Have you any fish?'

'Well,' Jack said, 'I've got some fish.' Jack put his hand in the slip bag on his back and took out a trout about three or four inches. He handed it to the young woman. She caught it.

'Here ye are, Hungry!' and she threw it. The eagle just 'kweek', snapped it like *that* and gobbled it up!

Jack said, 'I see it really is hungry!'

She said, 'Yes, Hungry is always hungry. But let's forget about him at the present moment; tell me something about yourself. Where did you come from?'

Jack told her, 'I came from the village about six or seven miles down the river. I stay with my mother, my father died. I don't remember my father very much. I stay with my mother there, who is very old, up in years. The only enjoyment I find is fishing. But it amazes me, young woman, where do you come from?'

'We come here very often,' she says, 'Hungry and me. I spend most of my time here.'

'Well,' Jack says, 'you don't mind me, if I start to fish?'

She said, 'Never mind fishing, let us talk!'

Jack wasn't interested in talking, he wanted to fish. But now Jack began to get the ice broken he began to feel a wee bit freer:

He says, 'Have you ever fished?'

'No,' she said, 'that's one thing I've never done in my life, is fish.'

So Jack put a couple of worms on the hook, cast it out in the pool and handed the young woman the rod. Just within minutes there was a nibble on the rope. She pulled it up and got a large trout, about four or five inches. She took it off, caught it and threw it at the eagle. The eagle 'wowk', gobbled it -- just while you wait!

So Jack said, 'Where did you get that bird?'

'Well,' she said, 'I got it from my grandfather many, many years ago. He gave it to me as a small chicken. And he's been with me for a long, long time, the only friend I really have.'

But Jack says, 'Where do you come from?' He began to get inquisitive.

She says, 'I come from the mountains. And I follow the river. I come here because I find solitude at the waterfall.'

But Jack said, 'There most be more things for you, a young woman, to do than coming here and spending your time at a waterfall!'

'Well,' she says, 'what's your name?'

And he told her, 'Jack.'

'Well,' she said, 'Jack, there must be more things for you to do than come here fishing by yourself!'

He said, 'I suppose that's true. But anyway, it's none of my business.'

She said, 'Are you working? Are you employed?'

Jack said, 'No, I work for myself. I've a vegetable patch; I grow enough to keep my mother and me alive.'

She said, 'Would you work for me? And I'll pay you well.'

'Well,' Jack said, 'it all depends on the work. I'm not interested in the money.'

She says, 'I want to escape!'

And Jack says, 'You? What do you want to escape from? You've got the world at your hands, you're a nice young woman!'

And Jack was still admiring those boots, you know. He'd never seen anything like them; they just fairly took his breath away. She was the most beautiful woman you ever saw, young and handsome.

She says, 'Have ye ever heard of the Ravens?'

Jack was amazed: 'The Ravens?'

'Yes – the Ravens – they are my uncles. Ever since my grandfather died I've been a prisoner of the Ravens, and I want to escape from them. But there's no way in the world I can get away from them without the help of someone like you. And if you're willing to come, help me escape from the Ravens and take me home to my mother's land across the mountains, I'll pay you exceptionally well.'

So Jack pondered for a wee minute: 'You want to escape from the Ravens – is it true that the Ravens really exist – is it true?'

'Yes, Jack,' she says, 'the Ravens really exist. But it's getting late. I'll have to make my way home or I'll be missed and there'll be a lot of trouble for me. Why don't you come here early tomorrow just before sunrise? Meet me here and we'll talk about it. I'll give you the problem; if you're willing to work for me you can say yes, and if you're not you can say no.'

'Fair enough,' says Jack.

And Jack never fished any more. He took a fish from his pocket and flung it to the eagle. The eagle 'lowhoop', snapped it up like that! And he bade the young woman farewell and he made his way up the path.

But he was really disturbed, you know, his mind was disturbed. He walked to his mother's house and didn't remember walking the path back. In his mind he was mixed up; he half believed her and half didn't believe her. He wanted to believe her and didn't want to believe her. He was a young man who didn't understand the problem he was faced with. He couldn't get back to his mother quick enough to tell her what happened.

But to make a long story short, he made his way and his mother was in the kitchen making a bite for him coming back. He came in, placed his fishing rod behind the door, hung it up, took the two-three fish he had and put them in a wee box, took his worms and emptied them back in the garden. That's one thing Jack would never do, leave worms to die; he put them back so he would get them another day. He washed his hands and came in. His mother had his supper ready for him.

Jack's sitting and eating very slowly, and his mother's placing these things before him. She says, 'Boy, what's bothering ye? How did the fishing go?'

'Oh, Mother, it went well. I had a nice day.'

Now he's afraid to speak about this, you know. After him telling his mother the Ravens were a fairytale, he is going to turn round and tell her he's got proof the Ravens are alive! He doesn't know how she's going to take it. He is an upset young man.

But she says, 'Eat up!'

But Jack couldn't eat. So he breaks down and tells her: 'Mother, I've made a fool of you many times.'

'Well, Jack,' she says, 'you never made a fool of me really. You've never done me nae harm. You've been a good laddie to me, taken care of me all my life, I don't know what I'd do without ye. Since your father died you've been a great laddie to me and I've no complaints to make.'

'I know, Mother, it's all right about that. The thing that bothers me so much, you know, is when you try to tell me a story or a wee tale I don't believe.'

She said, 'Jack, what are ye getting at, what are you trying to tell me?'

He says, 'Mother, tell me about the Ravens!'

'Well, Jack, there's no much to tell about the Ravens,' she said.

He says, 'Tell me every single tale about the Ravens!'

She says, 'What brought the interest in the Ravens? Have you been thinking a lot about this? Were you on their land or something?'

'Now, Mother, I want you to tell me every single thing ye ken about the Ravens!' said Jack.

'Well,' she said, 'eat up your supper and I'll tell ye.'

So Jack ate as much as he could, and told his mother he couldn't eat any more.

'Well, Jack,' she says, 'I'll tell ye: many, many long years ago when your father was only a young man and I was only a young lassie, there used to be an old man who came here every year from the mountains to shop in the village. He had a long white beard and he came every week to the village store. He lived on his own in the mountains and never talked to anybody. People called him the Hermit and said he worked with magic. They had many bad tales about him. Then a year passed and he never turned up; till one day he appeared. With him he had the two most beautiful boys ye ever saw in your life, identical twins they were! Dark, tall and dark, with long, straight noses and long, straight hair, as if they were foreigners. But they had beady glassy eyes. They never spoke. They paid attention to the old man, every word he said, and they obeyed his orders. And people began to get kind of curious about this; they asked him, who were the boys?

'He turned around and said, "Oh them – they are my Ravens – my Ravens!"

'Well, shortly after that these boys grew up, and the old man never came back any more. These Ravens grew up to be young men, started to thieve and steal across the country, robbed and stole because they had magical powers given to them from the old man. They could travel across the country faster than anybody else. But they say the big house on the hill where they live is full of plunder, and nobody is safe anymore as long as the Ravens are alive. All tried, everybody tried to capture and find some complaint about them, but they could never get anything on the Ravens. They still exist!

'And we never saw the old man anymore. But the Ravens never, never come here. The stories that we hear coming from the mountains – the Ravens are still as active as ever. And woe be to anyone who is caught between the boundaries of the Ravens' land; they are never seen or heard tell of again!'

And Jack was kind of worried: 'Ye know, Mother, I had a very funny experience today.'

'A very funny experience, son,' she says, 'what way?'

'Well,' he said, 'I travelled farther up the river than I've travelled before and I had the pleasure of meeting the most beautiful young woman I ever met in my life at the waterfall. She told me that the Ravens are her uncles, and she wants me to work for her.'

'No, Jack,' she says, 'don't do it, son! Please, for my sake, for your mother's sake, don't do it; have nothing to do with them, because you'll rue it for evermore. That old man, their grandfather or her father, whoever it was, nobody knows for sure, but he was a wizard. He gave them magical powers, and no one can do anything to them. But, who did you meet?'

'A young lassie, the bonniest looking young lassie that ever I saw in my life,' he said, 'and she's so beautiful it just took my heart away . . . Mother, you want to see her boots!'

She says, 'Jack, the question of boots, you're talking of boots: they tell me that the Ravens got boots with wings on them given to them by their grandfather, or by their old father who reared them up. They can travel hundreds of miles across the country and naebody can catch them. That's the way they escape on their thieving and plundering. They've got boots with wings on them and can travel faster than any human beings in the world – they're full of black magic. There's no way in the world you can do anything to them!'

'Well,' he says, 'Mother, I'll tell you the whole story. This young lassie I met says the Ravens are her uncles, and the old man was her grandfather. She wants me to meet her the morn at sunrise, and wants me to escape with her from the Ravens, take her to her mother's country across the mountains.'

'Jack, Jack, laddie,' she says, 'do ye ken what you're doing?'

'Well, Mother, I promised her I would do it!'

She said, 'Laddie, ye might never come back! You don't know what kind of people you're going among; the Ravens could end your days in minutes, the stories I've heard.'

'Well,' he said, 'Mother, I'll never rest in peace unless I do it. And I'm a man that keeps to my promise; tomorrow morning at sunrise I'm going back to meet her. And whatever she wants me to do I'm going to do it! There's nae other way, suppose I never come back! Mother, you've a few shillings collected, you've a few shillings that'll see ye through to the end of your days, use it for your ain purpose. If I don't come back there's no other way for me! I've made my mind up and I'm going, whatever happens, I'm going to take her away from the Ravens.'

'Well, Jack, Jack,' she says, 'I suppose there nothing I can say.'

'No, Mother, there nothing you can say that's going to deter me from what I want,' said Jack. 'I've made up my mind. Here am I as a young man now, almost nineteen years of age; I've stayed with you digging gardens and selling vegetables, fishing a wee bit in the burn. I've never seen life o' nae description and this is a challenge to me. I'm going tomorrow's morning.'

So the two of them sat and cracked for a long while. He got all the details about the Ravens and the cracks, some true and some untrue, you understand what I mean. It was folklore in some ways and truth in others. He sat and listened to his mother telling him the whole tale till it came near bedtime. And Jack bade his mother goodnight and he went to bed.

But he couldn't sleep. He tossed and turned the whole faring night, and in his mind he could see these boots, this beautiful young woman and this big eagle. It was coming sweeping down at him, the eagle making attacks at him, swooping attacks, but it wasn't touching him! And all in a minute when Jack saw it wasn't touching him – Jack lost his fear of the eagle.

But he wakened in the morning just as the cock crew. He got up, put on his clothes, went down the stairs, made a cup of tea for his mother and bade her goodbye. He never took his fishing rod or anything. He set himself back up the way he had come and followed the river on and on and on. Just as it was getting light, the sun was just coming up over the mountains when he landed at the waterfall. And sure enough, he made his way down the path that he'd taken before right to the very spot. There she was, sitting in the same place.

'A good morning, Jack!' she says.

'Good morning, young lady, good morning! You're here bright and early this morning; did you go home last night?' said Jack.

'Oh yes, Jack, I went home last night. And my uncles were very, very angry.'

'Now,' he said, 'tell me something before you start. I sat last night and had a talk to my mother; and she told me many funny, queer stories and tales. I want you to be honest with me and tell me the truth before we go another step.'

'Well, Jack, I'll be honest with you,' she said, 'and I'll tell you the truth.'

'What is it you want me to do?' Jack says.

She said, 'I want to escape from the Ravens!'

He says, 'How can I help you?'

She says, 'I'm going to tell you how you can help me. And you're the only one who can; I don't know anybody else who could help me.'

He says, 'What are the Ravens to you in the first place?'

She says, 'I'll tell ye a story if you'll listen to me. I came to stay with my grandfather, how and why I don't know. But I can remember a long time ago as a child leaving my mother's land and travelling on horseback over the mountains through darkness and through light and through storms; we landed in this big house to the comfort of my grandfather, whom I dearly adored. And when I landed there in my grandfather's house there were these two young men, whom I instantly hated for evermore! I knew they were no relation to my grandfather, because my grandfather didn't have anybody. By one word or another I tried to talk to my grandfather, and he told me that they were the Ravens, just Two Ravens. And to keep me occupied my grandfather got me an eagle, Hungry, as a chick; and told me that I would be safe as long as he was alive, that Hungry would take good care of me. But someday I would have to return to my mother over the mountains.

'My life as a young girl spent with my grandfather was very happy. The Ravens never bothered me very much, I was too young. But when I began to grow up and get mature they began to pay more attention to me. And my grandfather wasn't worried. One day I came home and found my grandfather seriously ill, he was dying. He made me promise to lead him by the hand to a secret burial ground where he would lie and rest for evermore, where no one would find him.

'And, Jack, this is the story I'm going to tell to you, and I hope it will never be repeated: my grandfather was a lonely old man who stayed up in these mountains by himself, who practised magic for many years. He had many trips to the village to buy supplies to keep himself alive, but one day he was walking along on his way to the village when two small ravens fell from a nest. They were high in a tree, and my grandfather being an old man had no way to put them back in the nest, he felt sorry for the birds. So he took them back home with him – this is the story my grandfather told to me.

'With his magic power he turned them into two boys and reared them up as his own. He thought they would grow up to be natural, nice and kind, but being ravens they could never do that! So, many years later he got word that my father had died, my mother was left on her own with me to take care of, and no way to look after me. He went across the mountains, collected and brought me back here, reared me up as his own; because Mother was his only daughter, and he had everything here under the sun to give me, money, love and freedom. The only thing he ever detested in his life was bringing the Ravens to life; many days he told me as he lay in bed that he wished from his heart he'd never done it!

'But he loved these boys dearly, although they didn't think much of him. He worked his magic and made them each a pair of boots with wings that would travel faster than sound. He also made them two rings to put on their fingers they could use when he was gone which, if it ever came to pass that they needed – they could change themselves into any form on the Earth – except a raven! Because, once they ever changed into a raven again there was no way back.

'Now, Jack, what I want you to do is to come home with me to my grandfather's home, collect my personal possessions and take me over the mountains home to my mother.

I'll pay you well if you're willing! But remember: I have one ring, which I have stolen from the Ravens, in my possession. They have only one between them – they can never, never split up because they need this ring. Both of them want to marry me! And the only reason that keeps them from falling apart with each other – as long as I own this ring – they can never be apart, having only one ring my grandfather gave them now. I want you to come and take me across the mountains from these Ravens who are no relation to me, whom I desperately hate!'

'Well,' Jack said, 'it's a queer tale, a very queer tale. There not much I can do about it. How would you chance to escape?'

She said, 'There are horses, plenty of horses; I think we should go on horseback. We can take the finest horses that the Ravens possess and ride, be well over the mountains before they discover us.'

But Jack said, 'If they've got so many magical powers they're bound to find us somehow.'

'How they find us, Jack,' she said, 'and what they do after they find us, is your problem. But I'm giving you the ring to use in any form that you require of it.'

And she took the ring out of her pocket, slipped it on Jack's finger:

'*Now, Jack, you can only use it three times to change into something different, and then it's no use except to change back.*'

'Fair enough,' says Jack, 'I'm willing!' He had made up his mind a long time ago.

So, to cut a long story short, they made their way back to the castle, to the big house. And when Jack landed at this big house there was stuff that you'd never seen in your life! The young woman, Marigold they called her, led him through the castle and showed him the plunder that was stolen from all over the land by the Ravens. They had more than they ever needed. But they were so greedy, they just collected, collected after each other – you know what ravens really are, they'll steal anything – and nobody could catch them!

So when she took him into the long kitchen Jack looked up: hanging on the wall he saw two pairs of boots with wings.

Jack said, 'That's the first thing! Have you got a knife?'

She gave him a large kitchen knife. Jack took it and cut the wings off the boots, threw them on the floor.

'Now,' he said, 'if they want to follow us they ain't gaunna follow us with boots!' He told her, 'Take off yours, your boots!'

She says, 'Why should I?'

'Take off your boots and get in your stocking feet!'

So the young woman took off her boots and threw them on the floor beside theirs: Jack had it all planned.

'Now,' he says, 'to the stables!'

Into the stables they went. And by sheer good luck the Ravens had left their two big horses in the stables.

Jack said, 'Gather all your possessions that you can find, pack them in the saddle bag and let's go! Upon my soul, I'll try my best to take you across the mountains!'

So Marigold hurried as best she could, collected all the personal possessions she could find, packed them in the bag and threw it across the horse.

By this time Jack had come out. He had saddled the two horses:

'Now,' he said, 'let's be gone!'

They closed the door quietly behind them and set sail, they rode across the mountains. They rode and rode and they rode. They were always looking back.

But by this time, when they were gone for about three hours, who should come home but the Ravens! They opened the large door and shouted for Marigold. They wanted to eat. They were back with all their plunder. There was nothing, not a soul in the house. Nobody. And they looked on the floor of the kitchen – saw their boots and the wings cut off – and Marigold's boots lying beside them.

They said, 'She's gone! We must find her!' They ran to the stables – the two large horses were gone – the Two Ravens said, 'Let's get after them!'

So they picked another two horses and they rode. They rode and rode.

One brother said to the other, 'What should we do – shall we change?'

'No,' said the other, 'let's ride in pursuit.'

So they rode and rode and they rode. But the horses that they rode were faster than the ones Jack and Marigold were on; they began to catch up.

And Jack looked back.

Marigold says, 'Here come the Ravens; they're behind us, Jack! What are we going to do?'

And they came to a brook. Jack said, 'They're just upon us. There's nothing we can do!'

And what jumped up right in front of them but a hare, a brown hare. And Jack said, 'Hares we may be!'

Just within seconds he and Marigold were two hares. Off they set across the moor!

When the Two Ravens saw this they stopped their horses, and said, 'Hares they may be, hounds we may be!' And the other rubbed his ring – two hounds set off after the two hares.

And the hares were off and the hounds after them at full tilt! They ran and ran and they ran till they came to a river. There was no way across.

The first thing Jack saw when he came to the river as he was sitting panting and Marigold was panting – a salmon 'fweet', jumping!

Jack said, 'Salmon we may be!'

Just before you could say another word he and Marigold were two salmon and down into the burn!

When the Ravens came to the river they said, 'Salmon they may be, otters we may be!'

Before you could say another thing they had turned into two otters, and they were off after the salmon.

The salmon were swimming but the otters were swimming faster. Marigold and Jack swam and swam and they swam till they couldn't swim any longer, till they came to a little bend in the river.

Jack said, 'Marigold, we must change once more!'

And they clambered up. The first thing they saw was a pheasant's nest. Sitting in the nest were ten eggs.

Jack and Marigold . . . twelve eggs in the pheasant's nest – they changed themselves into two eggs in the nest.

When the otters came up they looked around and saw the nest, and said, 'Eggs they may be, ravens we may be!'

They turned into two ravens to pick the eggs and started picking when there was a rush of feathers in the sky!

Right down on top of them came this great eagle – took one in each foot and shook them both. Within minutes the Two Ravens were dead. They had tried to change themselves, but there was no way they could go back.

So, Jack took the ring and turned himself and Marigold back to themselves once more. There was the nest and there was Hungry. There were the Two Ravens dead for evermore.

And he said to Marigold, 'You've no more worry about the Ravens, they're gone for evermore. There's no way in the world they can come back.'

'I knew a long time ago,' she said. 'Jack, you planned it well. If you had never turned us into those eggs, they would never have turned into ravens. What gave you the thought?'

He said, 'I had no thought. I just did it on the spur of the moment.'

'Well, it saved our lives. The Ravens are gone, now we can go back home and live in peace.'

So Jack and Marigold went and collected their horses, rode back to the castle and stayed the night together. The next morning they rode down and saw Jack's mother. They made arrangements to take Jack's mother away from the old house with them to the castle to live happy in luxury for evermore.

And Marigold says, 'Jack, now the Ravens are gone I am in no hurry to see my mother. After everything is settled and we're happily married we'll cross the mountains to see her. But Jack, come here!'

He says, 'What is it, darling?'

She said, 'The ring, give it to me!'

He says, 'What for?'

She says, 'Give it to me, Jack, because I want it!'

Jack took the ring off his finger and gave it to her. She said, 'Come with me!' and walked to the draw well. She caught it and threw it in the well.

He says, 'What did you do that for, Marigold?'

She says, 'Jack, I love you and you're my husband. You saved my life! I don't want you to turn into something that I wouldn't like you to be.'

And that is the end of my story.

# Jack and the Sea Witch

Once upon a time Jack lived with his mother in a wee cottage by the shore. His father had died when he was young and he was reared by his mother. And further along the shore lived his mother's old sister, his old auntie, in another house. Jack visited her frequently from time to time when he was a boy, and his auntie loved him as much as his mother did.

But all Jack's time he spent it on the beach, on the shores hunting the rocks and cliffs and fishing and doing everything under the sun, doing an odd bit job here and there to help his mother. And that's the way he grew up till he came to be a young man. His mother and his auntie adored him because he was such a good laddie. Till one day he came home and he was sitting after his supper, sitting very quiet.

He says, 'Mother . . .'

She says, 'What is it, Jack?'

He said, 'How can you catch a mermaid?'

'Laddie,' she said, 'you canna catch a mermaid. Mermaids dinna exist. They only exist in folk's minds. Sailors tell stories o' seein mermaids, but it's no really a *mermaid*.'

He says, 'Mother, I've seen a real mermaid. And I've been watchin her now for months. I've fallen in love wi her and I want to catch her.'

'Ach laddie, you've been dreamin! You fell asleep along the shore some place, the way you always wander on them rocks, and you've dreamed it.'

'No, Mother,' he said, 'I never dreamed it.'

'Well, I dinna ken,' she says, 'they tell so many tales about folk catchin mermaids. They say you can catch them and you tak off their tail and you can hide their tail or do whatever you can, but I dinna ken very much about it. But I'll tell ye, gang along to yer auntie and tak some bits o' messages down to her. I was going to send you down to her anyway. She's older than me and she kens an awfa lot mair than me about these sorts o' things. She's been all her days at the sea, and if there's anybody in the world can tell ye about mermaids and put that silly notion out o' yer head, maybe she'll help ye a wee bit.'

'Okay, Mother,' he says. And she could see by it he was kind o' worried.

So she packs a wee basket with bits o' things for her old sister, who was getting up in years, maybe in her seventies, gives them to Jack and Jack goes along the shore, his path to his auntie's.

And when she got him away, 'That silly laddie o' mine,' she says to herself, 'God knows, maybe he did see a mermaid. Ach, it's hard to believe, too, that there is such a thing as a mermaid. I heard his father, and a good sailor he was at one time, away for years, sayin that many's a man had seen a mermaid. They decoyed sailors awa. But ach, I dinna ken. Anyway, he'll forget it soon.'

But away Jack goes, travels along the beach to his old auntie's. The old woman stayed on the shore and kept ducks, looked after and kept nothing but ducks. Up he goes. His old auntie was pottering about the house when he landed.

'Oh it's yersel, Jack,' she said. 'How's yer mother keeping?'

'No bad, Auntie. There's two-three bits o' things she sent down to ye.'

'Aye, put them in there. And I'll come in and mak ye a wee mouthful o' tea.'

So Jack goes in, sits down at the fireside . . . and then puts a fire on for his auntie. She comes in, mutch on her head and a long frock on her. She sits down at the fireside and gives him something to eat.

'Ye ken, I'm no very hungry, Auntie,' he said.

'Jack, I ken you better than that, son. What's bothering ye?'

'Ach well, Auntie, tell ye the truth, ye'll maybe no believe me what I'm going to tell ye. But . . . I want to catch a mermaid.'

'What? Laddie, do ye ken what ye're sayin?'

'Aye, Auntie, I want to catch a mermaid and I dinna ken how to catch her!'

The old woman sat for a long, long while. She thought. She said, 'Laddie, did ye see a mermaid?'

'Aye, Auntie, I've seen a mermaid,' he said. 'I've been seein her now for months, all summer. And she comes into this wee narrow lagoon, but when I go down she escapes back through it and I've nae way in the world to catch her.'

She says, 'Laddie, ye ken, I half believe ye and I dinna believe ye.'

'But, Auntie,' he says, 'between me and my father in the grave, I'm tellin ye the truth! I've seen a mermaid.'

'Laddie, you've got to be careful what you catch in the seas round about here. There's many and many a thing that naebody kens that I ken. There's many a droll thing can be catcht in the sea! Well, if your mind's made up, there's only one way to catch a mermaid . . . you'll have to go and search for Blind Rory the Net-maker. And he'll mak ye a net to catch a mermaid if it's a mermaid you want. But I'm telling ye, laddie, for yer ain sake, ye're better to leave well alone! Oh, I've heard stories o' men catchin mermaids and hidin their tails and doin all sorts o' things, but never nae good come out o' it. It's ay bad luck! Oh, they're bonnie things when you see them, but they can also be a sheer lot o' trouble to you.'

'Auntie, I want to catch a mermaid!' he said. 'I've seen her, I love her and I want her.'

'Well,' said the old auntie, 'let you be your own judge. You go and search out Blind Rory.'

'But where am I goin to find Blind Rory?'

'Well, the last I heard o' him, he stays many, many miles awa fae here on the beach, him and his granddaughter. And he maks nets. He's the man to see! I dinna ken if he'll gie ye a net or no, or mak ye yin, or what ye can do. But for yer ain mind and for yer ain sense o' peace or justice . . . go back and tell yer mother what I tellt ye, to forget the whole thing! And leave well alone.'

'No, Auntie, there'll be nae peace for me till I catch the mermaid.'

'Well, well,' she said, 'son, please yersel. But I'm only advisin ye . . .'

'I ken ye mean well, Auntie, but it's gotten wi me that I get nae peace o' mind till I catch this mermaid.'

'But, son, what are ye goin to do with the mermaid after ye catch it?'

He says, 'Auntie, she's a young woman, the bonniest young woman I've ever seen in my life. And all she's got is a fish's tail – the rest o' her is perfect.'

'Ah,' she said, 'I ken. I heard my great-granny, your great-great-granny, telling me stories when I was a wee infant years ago that there were yin man that catcht a mermaid

wonst. And he was a sair punished man. So I'm advisin ye,
Jack, for yer ain good, to go back to yer mother and forget all
about it!'

'No,' he said, 'Auntie! I'm no goin to forget all about it.'

'Oh well,' she says, 'please yersel. Anyway, there a couple
o' dozen o' duck eggs. Tak them up to yer mother when ye
go back. And go and please yersel. Ye're a young man, ye're
twenty years of age and there's nae use o' me tellin ye
anything. Ye canna put an old head on young shoulders, so
you do what ye want to do and come back and tell me how
you got on. And if there's any help that I can gie ye, remember
I'm always here!'

'Right, Auntie!' he said. He bade her farewell and away he
went. He travelled back, back home and up to his mother.
Mother was in the house.

'Well, Jack,' she said, 'ye're hame.'

'Aye, Mother, I'm hame.'

'How did ye get on? Did ye see yer Auntie Maggie?'

'Aye,' he said, 'I seen her.'

'And what did she tell ye? Did she knock some sense into
yer head?'

'No, Mother, she never knocked nae sense into my head,
or she never knocked nane out o' it. She tellt me a lot o'
things, but . . . she tellt me, Mother, to gang and seek out
Blind Rory.'

'Aha,' says his mother, 'that's a job alane – seekin out Blind
Rory the Net-maker! Some folk says he works with the
Devil.'

'Well,' he said, 'if he works with the Devil surely he can
mak me a net. I'll pay him for it. I've a few shillings in my
pocket.'

'Well look, Jack,' she says, 'you're the only son I've got.
And since your father dee'd you're the only help I've ever

had. And I dinna want to see naethin comin ower ye. I couldna tak it if onything happened to ye. But if ye want to go and seek out Blind Rory ye'll have to travel into the next town and through that to the next town, fifty-odd miles awa fae here, places I've never been in my life. But anyway, the last I heard, my old sister tellt me that some wanderin sailor tellt her, that Blind Rory stays in some kind of cave, him and his grand-daughter, near some town.'

'Well well, Mother,' he says, 'I'll no get nae peace o' mind till I go and find out for myself.'

So next morning Jack got up early. His mother packed him a wee bundle of whatever he needed to carry him along the road, his coat and his bit o' meat in a bundle for himself. And he flung it on his back and away he goes. On he travels, he travels and he travels and on and on and on. Comes night-time he kindles a wee fire, makes himself a bite to eat and lies down to sleep at the back of a tree. He does the same the next day and the next day till he comes to the first town. And by good luck it is a fishing town. Jack never was here before, the place is all strange to him. And he sees an old man sitting on a summer-seat, a seat at the side o' the shore. He walks up to the old man.

'Excuse me, old man,' he said, 'I'm lookin for a man they cry Blind Rory the Net-maker. He's supposed to be no far fae here.'

The old man took a good look at him, scratched his head, 'Ah laddie, laddie,' he said, 'what are ye wantin Blind Rory for? I thought the likes o' you would hae mair sense to keep awa fae folk like that! Do ye no ken the legend that Blind Rory works with the Devil? All these shipwrecked sailors and things that's done in the sea, they say Blind Rory's the cause o' it. He wrecks boats and things for the sake o' gettin the stuff off them when they come in wi the tide.'

'Ach,' says Jack, 'I dinna believe them stories. I'll see for mysel.'

'Well, I'll tell ye,' says the old man, 'I'm an old sailor mysel. And ye'll gang on twenty-five mile to the next town, and when ye get there go down to the beach. And right close to the waterside ye'll come to a wee white house, and that's my old brother. Tell him I sent ye and he'll help ye!'

'Good,' says Jack, and he bade the old man farewell.

Away goes Jack and he travels and he travels and he travels on. He comes to the town and walks through the town, walks along the beach and he comes to the wee white house. He walks round to the front o' the house and there's an old bended man with a long grey beard sawing sticks at the front o' the house.

'Hello!' says Jack.

'Hello!' says the old man. 'What can I do for ye?'

'Well,' says Jack, 'to tell ye the truth, I've come from the neighbouring town and I met an old man who said he was your brother.'

'Oh aye,' he said, 'my old brother, oh aye. I haena seen him for years. But anyway, what have ye come to see me about?'

'Well, to tell ye the truth, old man, I've come to see ye – could ye help me?'

'Ah well,' says the old man, 'by the looks o' you, a young strong powerful man, ye dinna need nae help fae the likes o' me!'

'Ah but,' says Jack, 'the kind o' help I want, I canna do it for mysel. I want to ken where's Blind Rory.'

'Blind Rory?' says the man, 'What are you wantin him for? Ye ken it's even bad luck to speak about Blind Rory in this place, never mind gang and see him!'

Jack says, 'I want him to mak me a net.'

'Oh,' says the old man, 'he'll mak ye a net. He'll mak ye a

net, but it's what ye get in the net after ye get it! I ken many stories about folk that bought nets fae him here and ... droll, droll things happen to them. His nets is good, but it's what you catch in them ...'

'Well, that's what I want,' says Jack. 'I want a net to catch a mermaid!'

The old man says, 'What age are ye?'

'I'm twenty.'

'Oh, ye're twenty. What age do you think I am?' the old man says to him.

'Ah,' Jack says, 'ye're an old man about sixty or seventy.'

'I'm ninety! And I've seen an awfa lot o' mair years than you. And I'm telling ye, don't ever try and catch a mermaid! Because it's bad luck. Ye're too young to get bad luck at yer time o' life.'

Jack says, 'Look, old man, are ye goin to tell me or are you no goin to tell me where can I find Blind Rory? I'm no wanting nae mair o' yer stories. I'm sick with you and your brother and my mother and my auntie all tellin me the same thing! Can you no let me think mysel what to do for a while?'

'Well,' says the old man, 'you have it your way. Go along that beach there and go round the first big clift face to the second clift face, and then the third clift face you'll come to a bay. And somewhere in that bay – there's nae road to it – ye'll find a cave, and in that cave is Blind Rory with his grand-daughter.'

'Right,' says Jack.

'But I'm tellin ye, it's a long, long way and it's a sheer clift all the way, so you'd better watch yerself!'

'I'll watch mysel,' says Jack.

He goes back to the town and he buys two-three messages to help him on his way, and away he goes. He wanders on and he wanders on up this wee clift and down this wee clift, round this wee bay and through this wee path. He wanders here and wanders there till he goes round the first clift, round the second clift, round the third clift right down till he comes to the third bay, till he's that tired he has to sit down on the sand with his back against a rock. And he must have been sitting for about an hour when he sees this bonnie red-headed lassie with her hair down her back running down along the beach.

Jack saw her and he ran after her.

When she saw him coming she tried to make off, but he was faster than her and he catcht up with her. She turned around to him and she was like a wildcat.

She said, 'What do you want off me, leave me alone! Youse folk . . . we keep to wirsel, we don't want—'

'Wait, wait, wait, lassie,' he said, 'wait! I dinna want to do ye nae harm. I'm no here to touch ye.'

'Well, what do you want off me? I never interfere with nobody in this world, so leave us alone.'

He said, 'I want to see your grandfather.'

The lassie stopped, 'What do you want to see my grandfather for?'

He said, 'I want to get a net fae him.'

'Oh aye! Well if that's all ye want, you'd better come wi me.' So the lassie walked along the shore and he followed her up this path to this clift face.

She said, 'Stand there!' an opening hung with canvas in the face of the clift.

Jack must have stood for about five minutes and he heard arguing and chatting and speaking inside this big monster cave. He could hear the voices echoing away back into it. But anyway, the lassie came out, 'Ye can come in seeing you've come this distance.' In goes Jack.

When he landed inside this cave it was the same as if you were going into the biggest dining hall you ever saw in your life. This place was huge, just like a monster house. And it was all hung with all the fishing things under the sun, stuff that was salvaged from boats that went down. There were barrels and boxes and nets and creels and everything under the sun that was needed for fishing. And sitting on a stool in the middle of the floor beside this big fire was the biggest old man that Jack had ever seen in his life. And his hair was down his back and it was fiery red, so was his beard. And he was stone blind. When he spoke his voice rumbled right through the cave inside.

'What can I do for ye, boy?' he said. 'Come forward, boy, where I can hear ye closer. And what do ye want of me?'

'Well,' Jack said, 'I've come a long way. You're Blind Rory, known as Blind Rory.'

He said, 'I am Blind Rory.'

He said, 'I want to buy a net.'

'What do you want a net for, boy?' he said. 'To catch fish?'

'No,' says Jack, 'I don't want a net to catch fish. I want a net to catch a mermaid.'

'What?' says Blind Rory, and his voice, sure it echoed right through the cave. 'Boy, do you mean to tell me that you've come all this distance and ought to have more sense – a young man o' your age who would want to catch a mermaid? The best thing you can do, son, is go straight back the way you came and forget that you ever saw a mermaid!'

Jack said, 'Look, I've got money and I want to buy a net fae you. And you're the only person in the country that can give me a net.'

The old man said, 'Look, I'm telling ye: *if I give ye a net, whatever you get in it is yours.*'

'Well,' says Jack, 'that's what I want.

'But,' he says, 'what if ye get in it is *no* what ye want . . . ye'll have to keep it!'

'Well,' says Jack, 'that'll be up to me.'

'Well,' says the old man, 'if ye're persistent and you want a net, I'll give ye a net. But remember, what ye catch in it will be yours and yours only! And I canna gie ye nae help after that. But I'll give ye a net, I'll no charge ye for it, laddie. Ye've come too far. But ye willna tak nae advice fae me, and you've been well warned by your mother,' as Jack had tellt him about his mother and his auntie, and the old men of the village. 'And you will no listen. But I'm tellin ye again, the best thing you can do is forget about me, the net and the mermaid and go straight back as if nothing had happened to ye!'

'No,' says Jack, 'I want ye to give me a net to catch a mermaid.'

'Well,' says the old man, 'ye're really determined. Go over there to that wall.' And over Jack goes. He says:

'Shove your hand in that big canvas bag.'

Jack shoved his hand in the big canvas bag. And he pulled out this net, like a poke with corks on it round the top, like a long bag.

'*That*,' says the old man, 'is the net you want and I'm givin it to you free. You're the first man that ever come into this cave since ever I took over here, and I hope you'll be the last. But remember, the minute you take this net out o' this place you canna come back, or I canna give you no help. Whatever ye catch in it is yer own, or whatever ye get you must keep!'

'Well,' says Jack, 'that's what I want.'

'Well,' says the old man, 'we'll say no more about it.' He said to the lassie, 'Give him somethin to eat.'

The lassie gave him a good feed. They sat down. And he

never mentioned it no more to the old man, and they cracked a long, long while. Jack bade the old man and his grand-daughter goodbye, took his net in his pack and set sail for home.

He travelled and he travelled, on and on and on and on, travelled all the way back the way he'd come till he landed back in his mother's house. And his mother was surprised to see him.

'Well, laddie,' she said, 'ye've been away a long, long while.'

'Aye, Mother,' he said, 'but it was worthwhile.'

'Maybe,' says the old woman, 'maybe it was worthwhile, maybe it wasna. Did ye see Blind Rory?'

'Aye, Mother,' he said, 'I saw a lot o' folk. And they all gien me the same advice. What is it about the mermaid that youse folk dinna like?'

She said, 'Jack, ye're too young to understand.'

He says, 'I'm no young – I'm twenty years of age! And I'm bound to ken what I want – I want the mermaid!'

'Right,' says his mother, 'you go ahead and you catch your mermaid, but remember: ye paid nae heed tae naebody. So whatever happens to ye when ye get a mermaid and what ye do wi it is up to yersel.'

'Well,' says Jack, 'can folk no let it be that way and let me do what I want?'

So his old mother gives him his supper and he goes to his bed, and he takes the net with him in case his mother would destroy it. Up to his bed with him, puts the net below his head. All night he couldna sleep, he couldna wait till daylight, till he got back to the beach.

Now this place where Jack was supposed to see the mermaid was a long, narrow lagoon where the water came in, it was awful, awful deep. And there was a narrow channel in-between. And every time he seen her playing in this wee round pool, when he ran down to get close to her she escaped through the channel. And he made up his mind that he was going to get a net that he could set in the channel, so that when she went back out – she wouldna see it coming in – but he would catch her on the road back out.

Right, so the next day was a lovely sunny day and away he goes. He sets his net, and he sits and he sits and he sits, he sits and sits till it gets kind o' gloamin over dark and a mist comes down. He hears splishing and splashing in the water.

He says, 'That's her!' Then he pulls the string and his net opens up. And he runs down . . . 'sheook' – in she goes to the bag. He catches the bag and he sees the long hair, and the fish's tail and the hands, the face. He pulls the net tight and he flings it on his back. Then he makes back to his mother's house with it as hard as he could. But by sheer good luck who was up at his mother's house at the same time seeing his mother, because she wasna keeping very well, but his old auntie.

In comes Jack to the house: 'Mother, Mother,' he says, 'light the lamps!'

'What for, laddie?'

He says, 'I got a mermaid!'

The old woman was surprised, 'Mermaid, laddie,' she says, 'there's nae such a thing as a mermaid. I tellt ye that . . .'

'But Mother,' he says, 'listen! I got the mermaid and I've got her in the net, I got her in my net. Blind Rory's net did the trick – I got my mermaid!'

'All right,' says his mother, 'I'll light the lamps.' So his old auntie rose and she lighted the two paraffin lamps. And Jack dropped the net on the floor and shaked it out. He looked.

Sister dear, you want to see what he shaked out – an old

woman about seventy years of age! And every tooth the
length of my finger, and her two eyes staring in her head
and her hair straggly, and this fish's tail on her and her hands
with big long nails and them curled. And she's looking at
Jack, she's spitting at him. But she could speak as good as
they:

'*Aye,*' she said, '*laddie, you catcht me. You catcht me and I'm
yours and you'll keep me.*'

Now the old auntie who had come in about, she looked.
The old auntie gave one roar and she said, 'Laddie, laddie,
laddie, Jack! Jack, do ye ken what ye've gotten? You wouldna
listen to naebody.'

'Aye,' he said, 'I ken what I've gotten – I've got a mermaid.'

She says, 'Laddie, that's nae mermaid. You've got yourself
*a sea witch*!'

'What,' he says, 'Auntie?'

She said, 'You've got yourself *a sea witch*.'

'Aye,' says the old witch, 'you've got me! You've catcht me
in Blind Rory's net and I'm yours. And you'll look after me.
I'll do everything in my power to mak you suffer for what
you've done to me.'

'I'll take ye back to the sea,' says Jack, 'and fling ye in.'

'Na, na,' says the sea witch, 'that'll no do nae good!' She
spits on the two old women, Jack's mother and his auntie,
and her eyes are blazing at them.

The old women were that feart o' her they wouldna come
near her. So, she commanded Jack to do everything for her,
give her something to eat, make her a bed and do
everything:

'Now,' she said to Jack, 'Jack, every day you'll carry me to
the shore and you'll carry me back, and you'll let me bathe
and you'll wait for me. Ye'll tend me hand and foot for the
rest o' yer days! That's yer punishment when ye wouldna

listen: ye had no right settin a net and catchin me. I am a sea
witch. You shall be punished for the rest o' your days.'

Jack was in an awful state. He was sorry then. He said, 'I
wish I would hae listened to my old auntie and listened to
the old men and listened to Blind Rory.' But there was
nothing he could do about it now. He said, 'I'll fling her back
in the sea, Mother.'

'You mightna fling me back in the sea,' says the old witch,
'because I'll just be back here the next minute. And I'll go on
punishin you for the rest o' your days.'

'Well,' said Jack, 'so it may be, we'll see.'

'*We'll* see!' said the sea witch.

So Jack never got a minute's peace. Day out and day in she
made him do everything for her. She wanted the best of fish,
she wanted the best of meat, she wanted carried and a bed
made for her, she wanted everything done for her, she
wanted carried to the sea and carried back from the sea
twice a day. And the farther Jack was carrying her the
heavier she was getting. Till Jack got that weak he could
hardly move with her, and he didna ken what to do. He was
in an awful state.

The old auntie had banned herself from coming near
the house. And the old women hid themselves, they
couldna come near the sea witch.

Jack's mother tellt him, 'As long as it's in this house I'm
no comin back to the house. I'm goin off wi my old sister.'
The two old women cleared out and left Jack with the
witch. And he was in the house by himself.

But yin day he managed to get away by himself, and he
cut along the shore. The sea witch was sleeping, and he
made for his old auntie's house. He was out of breath from
running because he didna want to be long away. He landed
in and his old auntie was sitting.

'Oh, it's you Jack!' she says, 'what happened to you now? Where is she?'

'I think she's sleeping,' he said, 'till the sun goes down. Then I have to take her back to the sea. Auntie, ye'll have to help me! I'm sair wrought, I dinna ken what to do wi her. She's got me punished to death. When she shouts on me I carry her down the stair, because she canna move without a wet tail. When her tail gets dry I have to carry her down and back to the sea, keep her tail wet.'

'Well,' says the auntie,' you wouldna listen to me, would you? Nor you wouldna listen to Rory. But now you've proved your point. And you were well warned. But if ye ever get free o' this woman, this is bound to be a lesson to ye. But I'll tell ye, now listen to me and do what I tell ye tonight when ye get a chance: you'll go back up, Jack, and you'll tak her down when she wants down to the kitchen. Put her beside the fire for to gie her her supper. Once her back's turned to ye, ye'll snap off her hair wi yer mother's big shears. And ye'll mak a rope out o' her hair. Tie it round her middle and tie her hands and tie up her tail wi it – from her ain hair – and fling her into the sea, let her go to the bottom!'

'Right!' says Jack, 'I'll do that.' Back he goes.

But he was nae sooner coming in the door when he heard this roar, 'Are ye there, are ye there, are ye there?' This was the sea witch roaring, 'Come at once and carry me down!'

Jack ran . . . but before he went up the stairs he searched his mother's house, in the kitchen, and he got his mother's big pair of shears. He put them on the mantelpiece. Up the stairs he went and he carried this thing down with the long hair and the big long teeth, this sea witch. He put her sitting alongside the fire.

She says, 'Get me something to eat, the best o' fish, Jack!'

Oh, she wanted everything under the sun, it had to be everything o' the best.

But she was sitting eating. She could eat, ye ken, her two
hands were like any human being's, only for her tail.

Jack got round her back and he took the shears. He catcht
all her hair – oh, long hair, it was hanging on the floor – and
he snip, snip, snip, snipped the whole lot off. And she
screamed at him and swung round. If she had had feet
instead of a tail she would have torn him to ribbons. But
Jack kept out of her reach.

And she flapped and flapped and flapped and screamed
and carried on right round the floor, roaring and
screaming the worst way she could what she was going to
do to him. But Jack kept catching this hair. And he twisted
it into a rope, and jumped on top o' her, and he catcht her.
With the long hair he tied her two hands at her back, he
wrapped all this round her. And he put her across his
shoulder. She's screaming murder! And he carried her on
his back back to the lagoon. He flung her in! And down
she went. And he stood. The bubbles came up, bubbles
came up.

He must have stood for ten minutes and then he says,
'That's the end o' her. That's her finished.'

He was just going to turn and walk away when he sees the
bubbles coming back up again. And up from the water
comes this head, and looks at him. Jack looks and he sees the
bonniest mermaid that ever he's seen in his life, the original
yin that he saw the first time.

And she sat just within reach o' him. She came out, her
head out of the water and she spoke to him:

'Well, Jack,' she said, 'for a long while you've tried to catch
me. And ye ken what you've catcht. You've catcht a sea
witch. That's the end o' her. But ye'll never catch me because

I'll no be nae use to ye. The best thing ye can do is forget all about me, and never again – let that be a lesson to you – never, never try and catch a mermaid!' And she disappeared.

Jack turned round. He walked home and tellt this story to his mother. From that day on till the day that he went off the Earth, Jack never again tried to catch a mermaid.

And that's the last o' my story.

## La Mer la Moocht

Many years ago, in a faraway land, there wonst lived a fisherman, and him and his wife didna have any family. He stayed by the beach and all their life's work depended on what he could catch. Some days he caught very little and some days he caught a lot. When he caught a lot of fish his wife was very happy, but when he caught very little his wife was very upset. So it was very hard to please her because she was a very unpleasant woman. The poor fisherman loved her dearly and they didna have any children, so he tried his best every day to catch as much as possible.

One day he cast his nets and the sun was shining beautiful in a deep pool that he'd never fished before behind some rocks, wonderful rocks covered with seaweed. And he said, 'Today I must catch something!'

And then he pulled the net out. Lo and behold, he pulled . . . it seemed to be stuck in some way. He pulled it and he pulled it, but there was not one fish in the net. But he pulled it out – then it came up – a man was caught in his net, tangled, and his arms were through the net. And the fisherman pulled, and he pulled and he pulled. He was upset.

There in his net stood the most beautiful being he'd ever seen in his life – long golden hair, blue eyes – the most wonderful person he'd ever seen! The fisherman was aghast.

And he said, 'This is something that must be sent to me,' and he pulled the net in, took this person out of his net.

And the person seemed so very friendly. He was a man younger than himself, not more than a boy, about fifteen or seventeen years of age. And his fingers were beautiful, his nails and his hands were beautiful, his toes were beautiful and he was dressed in a suit of seaweed. The fisherman, who was way up in his thirties or forties, was so amazed. He'd heard many wonderful stories about mermaids, but never in his life had he ever seen a merman. And the merman just stood and looked at him with the most beautiful blue eyes he'd ever seen . . . and the fisherman was aghast. He thought, what shall I do with this person? Will I send him back in the sea or will I take him home with me? If I go back to my wife and tell her about this wonderful person I've caught in my net, would she be pleased or angry? Would she say, why didn't you bring him home and show him to me to prove to me that such a person exists, or is this another story because you've prob'ly fell asleep while you set your net and brung me home no fish? And the fisherman made up his mind he would take him home with him.

But the man he had took from his nets never said one single word. He just stood there as if he were carved of stone. And the fisherman took him by the hand and he led him. His hand was cold, as cold as if he were handling a fish. And he never said a word. The fisherman led him up across the shore-way. And he walked on his feet. The fisherman looked down; his feet were just like everybody else's but his toenails was as clean as clean could be.

And the fisherman felt a wee bit ashamed, a bit sad to capture such a beautiful person. He thought, I can't take this person back to my wife. But if I don't, she'll never look at me again. The young man he'd tooken from his nets had never said a word. When the fisherman had rolled up his net he'd just stood there. He didn't want to escape in any way. He didna want to run away – as if he would have been sent to the fisherman. And the fisherman had said to himself, 'I've caught many a fish before . . . I've heard of mermaids, but never in my life have I seen a merman.'

And now the sun came up, the sun was shining and the young man's hair begint to dry – and his hair was glittering like gold! And his seaweed dress begint to dry with the sun, and the fisherman fell in love with him. He couldna let him go, in no way would he let him go. So he had only one thing he could do . . . to bring him back to his wife.

He took him by the hand, led him along the beach and took him into his little cottage by the shoreside. When he led him in his wife was busy working in the kitchen. She was very poor.

She says, 'Have you got me something today?'

'Oh yes,' he said, 'I've got you something today.'

And his wife turned round, she looked. And there before her stood the most wonderful being that she'd ever seen in her life.

She says, 'Husband, what have you brought me?'

'Well,' he says, 'look, I've caught no fish today. But I've brought someone – I found him in my net.'

And the woman stood amazed before him: 'You mean to tell me you've—'

He said, 'Look, he . . . I found in my net. He was caught in my net, and I didna want to let him go because you wouldna believe me. I didna want to let him go, because I knew you would think I was wasting my time and cast my nets for nothing. But believe me, when I cast my net this morning this is what I found in my net – this man.'

She says, 'What is he?'

'Look,' he said, 'I don't know what he is, but he's never said a word since I took him.'

She said, 'Husband, he's a merman.'

'A merman?' said her husband.

'Yes, husband, he's a merman. But what are we gaunna do with him?'

'Well,' he said, 'you were always upset because I couldna catch enough fish to bring back to ye. But I brought this back I caught in my net today, and I fought a battle with myself: either let him go or to bring him back and come back to you who would scold me for catching nothing. If I told you what I had caught and let him go, you would never believe me.'

'Well,' she said, 'I'm glad you've brought him back. Bring him in and sit him down by the fireside!'

And by this time the seaweed vest that was on him begint to dry, and the more he dried the more beautiful he became. He became so beautiful that the woman . . . the tears were running down her cheeks to see this merman!

She says, 'Husband, this is the most wonderful being in the world!'

To his wife he said, 'Look, this is a merman. And, what are we gaunna do with him, in the name of the world, what are we gaunna do wi him?'

She says, 'We'll keep him to wirselfs.' She put on the kettle and made some tea. She offered him some.

His fingers was as good as your and my fingers, his feet was as good as your feet and his hair was the most beautiful of any in the world! And she gave him a bowl of tea. He took it in his hand and he drank it up. And then he spoke to them.

He said, '*I am La Mer la Moocht.*'

And the husband and the wife sat back by the fireside. He

said, 'Of course I can speak. I am La Mer la Moocht. I am the King of the Mermen.'

'You can speak!'

'You are the King of the Mermen?' said the fisherman when he found his voice. 'You are the King of the Mermen?'

He said, '*I am the King of the Mermen, and you have caught me. I am your prisoner. And it's up to you to do what you like with me.*'

The fisherman and his wife stood there aghast. And they *loved* him – anybody could love him. They were so amazed. They took him, they kept him and they taught him to say the words, spoke to him, and they loved him both. They were afraid to show him to anybody in case they both would take him away. He was just . . . out o' this world. And he was only about seventeen or eighteen years of age. They had never had any family and they just loved him by their heart.

Then one day, things was very bad with them. They had no more food left and no fish to sell . . . They couldna even let him sleep; when he fell asleep they sat beside him and watched him. When he fell sound asleep they sat beside him, and they were suffering without sleep theirselves! But they were afraid to let him go in case he would disappear, they were so much in love with him. They loved him so much they just couldna part with him . . . Till they got hungry and they got poor.

And then they turned round to him, they said one day, 'La Mer, we're poor.'

'I know,' said La Mer, 'you're poor.' He said, 'You want fish? I'll get you fish, come with me and I'll take you to fish.'

And the fisherman's wife said, 'If you're goin, I'm goin too!' She wouldna even let him out of her sight.

So the three o' them walked to the beach. And he took the net, said:

'Give the net to me!' and La Mer cast. He threw it out like *that*. And he clapped his hands. The net sank into the sea. 'Now,' he said, 'pull the net in!'

And they pulled the net – it was loaded with fish of all descriptions! Fish that the fisherman had never seen before in his life. There were more fish than they could ever use. And La Mer stood while they pulled the net in.

And the fisherman said, 'Look,' after they'd pulled, took all their fish, more than they'd ever need, 'we must sell some of these fish in the village.'

And La Mer, he never spoke very much, but he said, 'If you want to go to the village, then let's sell some fish!'

They pulled them in, hundreds o' fish in the net! They kept some for theirself and the fisherman packed up a bag o' fish, a large bag. And they walked to the village. Fish was in fair demand in these times.

La Mer said, 'I'll go with you!'

And the fisherman's wife said, 'Please, please, please, take good care of him!' He was so beautiful she just hated to see him go. But she said, 'Please, please bring him back!'

So, the fisherman and La Mer walked into the village. When he walked in the village he was tall and straight, so handsome that everybody looked. The fisherman was carrying the fish on his back, and everybody looked. Heads were turning every direction tae see this so beautiful man who walked with the fisherman. And they came to the market, they sold their fish. But lo and behold at that very moment, who should drive down through the village but the princess and her father.

She drove down through the village in her carriage and she's looking, she's waving to the people. The princess, the only daughter the king had ever had, and she passed by through the market where people were selling fish. The king was sitting, the footman was driving the carriage. And when she came there – who was standing – La Mer! He's standing beside the fisherman waiting to sell his fish. When lo and behold the princess espied him, she looked: there before her stood the most wonderful being she'd ever seen in her life! She demanded the coach should be stopped immediately, demanded that the coach be stopped!

And the footman stopped the coach, and the king said: 'What is it, my daughter?'

She said, 'Look, Father, look what I see! Do you see what I see?'

'No, my daughter,' he says.

'Look, Father, look, look! What do you see – who's standing there by the place selling the fish – have a look!'

And the king looked: he saw a person that he'd never seen before in his life, the most wonderful person in his life. And the daughter couldna wait.

She jumped out, she ran down to La Mer and she stood before him, said, 'Who are ye?'

He says, '*I'm La Mer la Moocht.*'

She said, 'Who owns ye? Who was yer father? Who are ye, where do ye come from?'

He said, 'I come from nowhere, I come from the sea. And I'm here with my friend the fisherman.'

She says, 'Come with me!'

By this time the fisherman had stood up and he said to the princess, 'Look, Your Majesty, this is my friend and we are fishermen. We are very poor. Can we please go home? We don't want to interfere with you in any way.'

She says, 'I must have this man, I must have this man!

Come to me – come up to my palace tonight. And I want to see you once more. I want to see ye wonst more. I *love* that person!'

And the fisherman said 'So do all we, *so do we all*.'

'Please,' said the princess, 'I haven't much time to wait. My father's anxious to get on. But give me your promise you'll bring him here tonight!'

And the fisherman said, 'I'll be there.' But he never said he would bring La Mer.

So the fisherman and La Mer walked home with all the money they got from the fish. He took him home. And his wife was very pleased. They bought many things on their way home for his wife. La Mer never said a word. And the fisherman turned round. He says to his wife:

'Look, we'll have tae do something about La Mer. We cannae send him off to the princess, she's in love with him.'

And his wife said, 'I'm in love with—'

He said, '*I'm in love with him too*! I am in love with him too! We can't send him off. If we send him to the princess we'll never see him again. What are we gaunna do?'

And his wife said, 'We love him. We don't want to hurt him.'

And La Mer said, 'I know yer problem. I don't want to go and leave youse; I don't want to go to marry a princess. Come with me back to the sea. Come with me and set me free!'

And his wife said, 'Please, take him back and set him free.'

So La Mer and the fisherman walked back to the same rocks where he catcht him. He said, 'La Mer, you're free. Go, La Mer!'

And La Mer turned round, said, 'Won't you come with me, old man? Come with me to the sea. I'll take ye to a place where you will never need to fish anymore, where there are diamonds and pearls, where the land – you will be free – where everything is a wonderful place.'

He said, 'I couldn't leave my old wife.'

'Walk with me,' said La Mer, 'please, come with me! Just put your feet in the sea and I'll take you with me.'

'I'll walk with ye,' said the fisherman. 'I'll see you off, because I don't want tae give you to anyone. Because we love you dearly.'

So the old fisherman walked into the sea with La Mer behind the rocks. And then lo and behold La Mer turned round. He catcht the old fisherman by the hand – he held on to the fisherman's hand.

'Come with me!' said La Mer. 'Please, come with me – you have been good to me and you treated me so square and so wonderful. Please, come and join me in my land, come, please . . .'

And the old fisherman went in to his waist. Then the old fisherman went up to his neck, then the old fisherman went up to his head and the water came into his eyes. But La Mer just was like a fish and the water didna seem to affect him any way. But the water is gaun into the old fisherman's neck and he begint tae feel that he wis drownin. He said, 'Please, La Mer, please, La Mer, let go your grip! Ye're far too strong for me!'

'*Come with me!*' says La Mer, '*and I'll take you to the bottom o' the sea, where you'll never need to worry, where everything is free!*'

'Please, please,' said the fisherman, 'let go your grip. Ye're far too strong for me.'

And then La Mer let go his grip. The old fisherman walked back to the shoreside and La Mer was gone. He walked home and he told his wife.

She said, 'Where is La Mer?'

He said, 'La Mer is gone . . . fir evermore, but someday I'll gae back tae the sea.'

She says, 'Look husband, if you go back to the sea, *will ye take me with you*?'

And that is the end of my story.

# Woodcutter and the Devil

A long time ago an old woodcutter lived in the forest and he cut timber for a living. He took it with a little handcart to the village to sell it to the local community. His wife had died and left him with three little boys, and he loved these children from his heart. But oh, he missed his wife terribly. Every evening when he'd put the children to bed he would sit there lonely by the fireside, put some logs on, and say to himself, 'I wish she was here to direct me and tell me what's to happen in the morning. Well,' he said, 'there's nothing else for it, I must rear the boys up the best way I can.'

Before they were school age the poor woodcutter took them with him to the forest and showed them how to work in the wood. They helped him lifting axes and doing things around the forest. Then at night time he took them by his feet by the fireside and told them stories, many stories.

So one day the oldest of the boys turned round and said, 'Daddy, I love your stories. But can you not tell us about something else? There are many other wonderful things, Daddy, to tell us than stories about trees and wind and windblown trees.'

'Son, I would love to tell you other stories, but me telling you about something else would make you far too inquisitive, to want to understand about things out in the world which you're not fit for.'

'But Daddy, we don't want to stay here and be woodcutters. We don't want to grow up like you, to be an old man spending your life in the forest cutting trees and getting no richer or no better off.'

'Well,' he said, 'I've tried my best, boys. I've brought you up and worked hard for you.'

'But Daddy, this is not a life for us – we want to be someone special! Daddy, tell us what to do!'

So he went into the forest and cut trees as usual. And he sat down there by himself.

'Isn't it terrible,' he said, 'my wife is gone, gone forever. And I'm left with three little boys. They're getting so grown up I don't know what to do with them. I'll never make enough money to give them an education or anything. They're so inquisitive and they want to understand so many things . . . *God Almighty, could you help me?*'

But no thought came to his mind.

He said, '*Jesus Christ, could you help me?*'

But no thought came to his mind.

He said, '*Would the Devil o' Hell help me? I would give my soul to the Devil this night if I had money to give my boys a good education!*'

And then there was a rumble o' thunder, it got dark.

He said, 'I'd better get up and make my way back.'

But lo and behold there before him stood this tall, dark man dressed in a long cape, 'I heard you, old man,' he said, 'I heard you!'

'Well,' he said, 'I was speaking out aloud, I was cursing to myself.'

'Oh, of course,' he said, 'you were cursing. But you mentioned my name.'

'Did I? And who are you?'

He said, 'I am the Devil!'

'The Devil?' he said. 'At last *someone* has come to help me!'

'Of course,' said the Devil, 'I've come to help you. Your God wouldn't help you, your Jesus wouldn't help you, would he? But I'm the Devil and I've come to help you. What is it you want?'

'Well,' said the old woodcutter, 'you know what I want. There's me, my wife's dead and gone to Hell or Heaven, I don't know.'

'Well,' the Devil said, 'I never saw her.'

'Well,' the old man said, 'she must be in a better place. Look, I've three grown-up boys and they're getting kind of inquisitive. They want a better life, they don't want to spend their lives with me in the forest. How can I give them a better life? I'm only a poor woodcutter making a few shillings to get food for them.'

The Devil says, 'I can help you.'

'Oh,' he says, 'I wish you would help me . . . Devil o' Hell, would you help me?'

He says, 'I'll help you. What do you need?'

'Money! I need money. I want to put them off to school, to college. I want to make men of them so's they'll grow up and be great men.'

Devil says, 'No problem. I'll give you all the money you want. But what have I to get in return?'

'Oh Devil,' he says, 'you can get anything you want of me. You can have *me*!'

Devil says, 'Is that true? Can I have *you*? Can I have you – heart and soul and body?'

'Devil,' he said, 'you give me money and you can have anything you want!'

Devil says, 'Go back home tonight, go to your kist in your bedroom – it will be full – but I'll be back for you in ten years' time.'

'Done!' says the old woodcutter. 'No problem, you can have me, heart and soul. By that time my boys'll be grown up and be young men, they'll not need me anymore.'

True enough. He wanders home a happy old woodcutter. When he lands home the boys have a few vegetables and a little meat on the table. They'd cleaned the house up, you know. And he had a little bite to eat. He walked in to an old kist that he had in his own room, and he lifted the lid . . . it was full of old clothes and things. He pulled the old clothes apart and there in the bottom it was packed with gold sovereigns.

He said, 'The Devil has told the truth. Now I have the money!' So naturally he called his three boys together and he said, 'Boys, listen: last night we had a discussion and you wanted to be great men. So I'm going to pay for you, I'm going to send you off to school. What would you like to be?'

So the oldest one said, 'Well, Father, I would like to be a minister. Because I know, Father, you lost my mother and I want to preach the word of God to all the people.'

'Is that what you want to be?' says the father.

'Yes, Father.'

'Well, a minister you can be.'

So he called the second son before him and said, 'What would you like to be, my son?'

He said, 'I would like to be a doctor.'

'Oh, no problem, son! I'll put you to college, I have plenty of money to put you to college now.'

'But Father,' he said, 'how have you become so rich?'

He says, 'Son, don't you worry about it.'

And to the youngest one he said, 'What would you like to be, my little son?'

He said, 'Father, I've talked to you and you've given me some very interesting discussions, and I would like to be a lawyer.'

'Well, son, no problem! You shall be a lawyer.'

So the next day the father, the old woodcutter, made arrangements to send his three young sons off to college wherever they wanted to go. He sent them off, paid all their expenses and lived by himself. And one became a great minister. And one became a great doctor. And one became a great lawyer. Nine years had passed. Now the boys were grown up. And one evening there was a knock at the door.

The oldest son came in. He said, 'Father, I have come to visit you.'

'Oh,' he said, 'my son, I am pleased that you have come to visit me. Because you know I haven't got long to go.'

'Why not, Father?'

'Well,' he said, 'it's a long story. Because you see, son, I sold my soul to the Devil just for the sake of you. And he'll be coming for me tonight.'

'Oh dear, Father,' he said, 'we don't want to lose you – you're our father and you've done so much for us. Do my brothers know about this?'

'No, your brothers don't know about this.'

He said, 'When is he coming?'

'Well,' he says, 'tonight at twelve o'clock.'

He says, 'Father, can I wait?'

'Oh,' he says, 'I don't want you to meet the Devil, son – you're a minister! You could never meet the Devil – he's coming!'

'Father,' he says, 'can I wait?'

But they sat and they talked till twelve o'clock. And lo and behold there was a rattle of thunder and a rattle at the door – in walks the Devil.

He said, 'Okay, old man, get up – I have come for you!'

And the minister got up. He had his crucifix hanging by his neck. 'Just a moment,' he said, 'you know this is my father.'

'I know,' said the Devil, and he held his hand before his eyes. 'I know,' he said, 'I know, I've come for your father.'

'Well, look,' says the minister, 'you know I preach the word of *God*!'

'Don't mention that word to me,' says the Devil, 'I don't want to hear it.'

'Well, look,' he says, 'I have never seen my father for many years. For my sake . . .'

'Not for *your* sake,' said the Devil, 'in any way! I've come for your father.'

'But I have never had time to spend with my father. Could you give him another year just to please me?'

The Devil said, 'Right. Look, if you take that thing from your neck so that I can talk to you, I'll think about it.'

So the minister turned his crucifix to the back of his neck.

'Now,' he says, 'we can look at you. I'll tell you: I'll give your father one more year just because you've been away for a while. But then I'm coming for him!'

'Okay,' said the minister, 'I'll make my peace with my father before that time.'

And then the Devil was gone.

So the minister and his son, they had a nice time together. And the minister went back to his parish. He stayed in the parish, left his father alone.

But a year had nearly passed. Then came the next son, the doctor, to visit his father.

They had sat there talking and discussing things when lo and behold there was another rumble of thunder. And the door opened – in walks the Devil again.

Doctor said, 'Who is this, Father?'

'Oh, it's an old friend of mine,' he said, 'son. He has come to see me. You know I have a long story to tell you, but I can't tell you right now.'

'But, who is it, Father?'

He said, 'It's the Devil.'

'The Devil?' said the doctor.

'Of course,' he said, 'the Devil, son. Look, all thon money I put you through college with didn't belong to me. It belonged to the Devil. And I've sold my soul to him and he's come for me. He's taking me tonight!'

'Oh,' the doctor said, 'so he's taking you tonight. Well, we'll have to see about this, Father.'

The Devil spoke, 'Old man, the time has come. I've given you one chance and no more!'

So the doctor son stood up. He said, 'Look, Devil, I know who you are – you're *the Devil*!'

'Of course I'm the Devil,' he said, 'I've come for your father.'

'But you can't take my father!' he said.

'But your father has sold his soul to me. I gave him my money – how do you think you got to college to be a doctor? How do you think you've saved so many souls . . . I'm angry about you! You have saved people that I could have had.'

'Well,' the doctor said, 'that's my business. I've been working hard.'

'You're a nice, sensible young man; you've been working hard, that's true,' said the Devil.

'But anyway,' he said, 'look, could you give my father one more year? My youngest brother of all comes back next year

– he is just about to become a lawyer. And if you took him away now, my youngest brother would be upset. Please, Devil, would you give my father one more year?'

'Okay,' said the Devil, 'one more year – no more!' Like *that* the Devil was gone.

So then the woodcutter and his son spent a lovely night together. But he had to go back to his practice, you know.

So another year passed by. The old man was quite happy by himself. And then there was a knock at the door and in came the youngest son.

He says, 'Father, at last! That's it – I am a lawyer now, Father!'

And his father was so happy to see him. He threw his arms around him and cuddled him. He said, 'My baby, my youngest son! You've really made it.'

'Yes, Father,' he said, 'I have. Let's go in and have a dine together and have a drink together.'

'But he said, 'Son, do you know what the time is ... tonight I can't spend much time with you.'

'Why, Father? I've come all the way to see you – aren't you happy to see me?'

'Of course, my son!' he said. 'I've had your brothers here, they've gone after their visits. Now you have come. But I can't spend much time with you.'

'Why, Father? Why can't you spend time with me?'

'Well, son, it's a long story. You know all that money I put you through college with? It was not mine. It belonged to the Devil.'

'The Devil?' said the lawyer.

'Of course, son,' he said, 'I sold my soul to the Devil to get you through college. And tonight he's coming for me.'

'Father,' he said, 'Father, I've not time to spend with you?'

'Well, son, this is the last chance! Your brother had a

chance and your second brother had a chance, and now it's
your turn.'

'But Father,' he said, 'I just can't let you go away with the
Devil – I've only just come here!'

They sat and talked, and then there was the rattle of
thunder again! And the door opened – in walks the Devil.

Rubbed his hands together, he said, 'Okay, old man, no
more chances. Who's this you have here with you?'

He said, 'This is my son.'

He said, 'A son?'

Yes, this is the son who has just come through college; he's
a lawyer.'

'Oh, he's a lawyer?' says the Devil. 'Well, they tell me
lawyers are very clever.'

'Well,' says the woodcutter, 'he's a clever young man.
Lawyers *are* very clever!'

So the lawyer turned. He said, 'I heard the story, Devil,
and about the extensions you gave my other brothers. Look,
I've only come back for a wee while to see my father. We
haven't much time . . . you can't take him away from me!'

'Well,' the Devil said, 'I gave your two brothers one chance
each. And it wouldn't be fair for me – even the Devil – to not
give you a little chance. How long would you like your
father to stay with you?'

'Oh,' said the lawyer, and he walked over to the table.
Burning on the table was a candle and it was burnt nearly to
the bottom. He said:

'Look, Devil, I know you've been kind. You've been more
generous than anyone, even more generous than God. You
gave my brother a year and you gave my other brother a
year. And all I'm asking you, Devil, can I spend a little time
with my father – until that wee bit of candle burns to the end
of the wick?'

'Oh,' the Devil said, 'certainly, no problem, no problem. That's not too bad, you can have your wish!'

And the lawyer walks up and he blows out the wee candle. He puts it in his pocket.

And the Devil is furious. He says, 'A minister could not beat the Devil and neither could a doctor. He said, '*It only takes a lawyer!*'

# Patrick and Bridget

Now you're not going to believe this story ... it's the strangest tale you ever heard in all your life; you will never again hear another one just like this! You won't find this in any book, suppose you paid a million pounds for it. And it all began a long time ago in Ireland.

You see, it came a certain time in Ireland known as the Iron Winter. For four long solid months it was frost and snow non-stop. Now everything was frozen solid, the sea was frozen, the Earth was frozen, the birds had died in the trees, people were poor, they had no food in their homes. The only thing they had in their homes was plenty of peats for the fire, the turf they cut during the summer. They had a big stack of peats, but there was not any food in the houses, no one had any food, because it was the Iron Winter and it was after the potato famine. Now, you're not going to believe this story, but it's true!

My story takes you to a little cottage not far from a small village, and there in this small, rundown cottage lived an old man called Patrick and his old wife Bridget. Now Patrick and Bridget had been married for fifty long years, and of course Patrick had tried his best to survive through the years. And they had survived the best way they could. But Patrick had one thing no one else had – Patrick had a big long nose, longer than anyone else's nose.

But because it was such an iron winter there was no food in the house. Patrick, he would sit by the peat fire with his pipe with his bare feet and his big, tackety, hobnail boots by his side, and he would sit smoking his pipe by the fire with his long nose up the chimney. And of course Bridget would sit there in the little kitchen and she'd wash the pots, she'd wash the spoons and ladles and knives over and over and over again. Till one morning, things were about to change.

Here was Patrick sitting by the fire smoking his pipe and Bridget had washed the dishes for the fifth time. No food. And turning she looked at Patrick and she said, 'Patrick, for the love of God, man, would you take that ugly face out of this house and don't bring it back!'

Patrick says, 'What's gone wrong with you, Bridget?'

She says, 'What's gone wrong with me, Patrick? There's never been food in this house for the last three weeks and you sit there with your ugly face smoking that pipe. Now take your ugly face out of this house and don't bring it back till you get me something for the pot – let it be fish or fowl!'

'But Bridget, there's nothing out there, the whole world is dead. There's not a fish or a fowl to be found! Where am I going to get you something for the pot?'

She said, 'You take your ugly old face out of this house and you won't bring it back till you get me something for the pot!'

And she caught his tackety boots and she threw them out in the snow and pushed old Patrick out in the snow with his bare feet and locked the door. There stood Patrick trembling with the cold.

But he pulled on his big hobnail boots and he laced them up and he stood there and he knew in his own mind Bridget would never let him back in the house until he found her something for the pot. Where was he going to get it? Everything was dead, the birds were gone, there were no rabbits, no pheasants, no nothing! No fish, the seas were frozen. And then he remembered a few days before he'd heard that a new priest had come to the little village near where he lived. And in those bygone days all priests were allowed to have a gun to shoot something for theirself for the pot. And Patrick thought if he made his way through the snow to the village, went to the old priest and borrowed the priest's gun, maybe he could shoot something with the gun, something he could give to Bridget to get his ugly old face back out of the cold and back to the fire. Anyway, this is what he did. He walked through the snow up to his knees till he came to the village and he walked up to the priest's house and he knocked on the priest's door.

Now, even though he was a new priest, he was a very old priest. And he came to the door and he said, 'Well, young man, what can I do for you?'

Patrick said, 'Father, it's my wife.'

'Oh dear,' said the old priest, 'what's wrong with the dear lady?'

Patrick said, 'Nothing wrong with her tongue, Father. She put me out of the house and told me not to bring me ugly old face back till I get her something for the pot.'

'Oh,' said the old priest, 'that's a terrible thing for a woman to do to her husband in weather like this in the cold snow. You'd better come in!'

So he brought Patrick into his house. He said, 'What's your name?'

'My name is Patrick, Father.'

'And well, Patrick,' he said, 'what would you want me to do for you?'

'Father,' he said, 'they tell me you have a gun.'

'Oh yes, Patrick,' he says, 'I have a gun. But it's a very, very old gun, it's an old muzzle-loader. Have you ever fired an old gun in your life, Patrick?'

'No, Father,' he said, 'to tell you the truth I've never fired any kind of gun in my life.'

'Well, Patrick, I have a gun but it's very, very old and you have got to be very, very careful how you load her. But I'll lend her to you and I'll show you how to use her.'

And you're not going to believe this story, but it's true. So off he went and he came back with an old brass gun, an old brass muzzle-loading gun and two little bags and a rolled up paper and under his arm he had an old stick mounted with brass.

'Now,' he said, 'Patrick, this is the gun. And the first thing you do, you'll hit it against your leg and you'll knock off the dust from the old barrel. And under my arm here I have a ramrod and here are two little bags, one of powder and one of shot. Now the first thing you do after you've hit it against your leg and knocked off the dust, you'll pour the powder down the barrel, and then you'll take a piece of rolled paper and from under your arm you'll take this ramrod and you'll stuff it down the barrel. And then you'll pour in the bullets – this is going to get your ugly face in out of the cold – and you'll stuff another bit paper in it, put the ramrod back under your arm. But for the love of God, Patrick, and all that's holy, don't pull the trigger of the gun with the ramrod still in the barrel or I won't beholden what will happen to you! Now you remember!'

'Yes,' says Patrick, 'I'll remember! You hit it against your leg, pour in the powder . . . thank you, Father,' and off he went.

But Patrick walked through the snow along the hedge-rows and sideways and byroads but he could not see one single soul, not a bird of any kind or a rabbit. And he's still thinking, 'Hit it against your leg, pour in the powder . . .' Patrick got a little mixed up in his head. But he searched far and wide, he could see nothing to shoot. And then he remembered, not far from where he lived was a large mill-pond, and from that millpond ran a river. The millpond was surrounded with reeds and Patrick had seen a few ducks there during the spring and the summer. Thinking to himself, 'If I made my way to the pond, maybe there'll be a duck on the ice and I could get just one single duck to give old Bridget to get me ugly face back out of the cold.'

So he made his way to the millpond through the frozen solid reeds in the pond with the gun under his arm, the two bags in his hands, and the ramrod under his arm. And through the ice he went and then he stopped for he heard a strange sound. The sound he heard was 'quack-quack-quack-quack'. Patrick looked through the ice and sure enough sitting on the ice were two big fat, plump ducks.

'Well upon me soul,' says Patrick, 'if I could get one of you for my old Bridget it would get my ugly face back out of the cold.'

And quickly he began to load the gun. He poured in the powder, he put the ramrod, he stuck it in, and the bit paper he's stuffing away . . . but he must have made some kind of noise for the ducks heard him and they got up off the ice and they started to fly. But instead of flying away, they flew towards Patrick while he was still loading the gun, and they flew overhead and Patrick was so excited he pulled the trigger – forgetting to take out the ramrod from the barrel of the gun.

There was an explosion that was heard all over Ireland! The gun flew from his hands and Patrick was catapulted backwards, and fell in a big bush of snow. And there he lay.

'Well, upon me soul,' says Patrick, 'what happened? Now

I'll never get me ugly face back in out of the cold, I'll never get something to Bridget, I'll die with the cold tonight, she'll never let me in.'

And there he lay in the snow. And then he felt something warm under him in the snow. He put his hand down through the snow to the bush where he had fallen. And lo and behold, what do you think had happened? Patrick had fallen on the top of a big brown hare that was asleep under the snow and broke its neck, and killed it instantly!

'Well upon me soul,' says Patrick, 'and all that's holy, is this not me lucky day? A big brown hare! This'll put a smile on old Bridget's face for the rest of her life. There'll be jugged hare, potted hare, hare soup for a full week. Am I not the lucky one?'

And then he put his two hands together to thank his God when he looked up in the sky – what did he see? For the ramrod had flown from the gun, went through one duck and through the other duck and was coming twirling down like a propeller and crashed into the ice.

'Well, upon me soul,' says Patrick, 'and all that's holy, is this not me lucky day? First a big brown hare, now two fat ducks! Will this put a smile on old Bridget's face for the rest of her life!'

Now I told you Patrick had big tackety boots on, didn't I?

So Patrick picked up the hare, put it in his bag and he walked out on the ice to retrieve the ducks. To the middle of the ice, there he picked up one duck. Oh, it was fat and plump! Into the bag. Pulled off the other duck off the ramrod, into the bag and then he tried . . . what do you think had happened to the ramrod? The ramrod had gone down through the ice and pierced the head of a ten-pound salmon lying under the ice, and killed it instantly!

'Well upon me soul,' says Patrick, 'is this not me lucky

day? A big brown hare, two fat ducks and a salmon! This'll put a smile on old Bridget's face like a baby for the rest of her life.'

Now I told you he had big tackety boots on. So, he began with his tackety boots to crack the ice, the thick ice. Pieces of ice were flying all over. And a piece of ice flew up and cut off Patrick's head and his head fell on the ice. But Patrick was a quick-thinking man; he grabbed his head and put it back on! And because it was so cold it stuck! Froze solid. Patrick tried it once or twice and it worked.

'Well, upon me soul,' says Patrick, 'is this not me lucky day?'

So he managed to retrieve the ramrod and the salmon and he put them in his bag. Picked up the gun and walked home. When he got back to the little cottage there was old Bridget standing at the door with her face like a prune.

'Where have you been, Patrick, all day long? You've been gone a long time. Did you get me something for the pot, fish or fowl?'

Patrick said, 'Bridget, me love, me doll of all Ireland, me love, I have something for you, you won't believe me!'

'Well,' she says, 'what have you got?'

He showed her the bag.

'Patrick' she said, 'me love, that's a hare!'

'Yes,' he said, 'me love, me doll of all Ireland, it's a hare and it's all for you!'

'Oh Patrick,' she said, 'are you not the hunter! I knew you could do it. You'd better come in out of the cold!'

Patrick said, 'Just a moment!' He showed her the bag.

'Patrick, that's a duck!'

'Yes, me love of Ireland, it's a duck! And it's all for you.'

'Well upon me soul,' says Bridget, 'are you not the great hunter? You'd better come in out of the cold. Now build up the fire, you can smoke your pipe to your heart's content!'

'Just a moment,' says Patrick . . .

'Another duck!'

'Yes, me love, another duck and it's all for you.'

'Oh Patrick, we will eat like kings, we will dine as kings and queens! We will have roast duck, we'll have jugged hare, potted hare, hare soup, roast duck and hare soup for a full week. You'd better come in out of the cold.'

'Just a moment!' said Patrick. 'There's something better . . .'

'Patrick,' she said, 'a salmon!'

'Yes, me love of all Ireland, it's a salmon and it's all for you.'

'Oh Patrick, are you the hunter, are you the fisherman! Salmon is for the gentle people. We've never had salmon in this house in all the years we've been married. You'd better come in out of the cold and I'll build up the fire and you can smoke your pipe for a week! And I will never say another word.' So she brought Patrick in out of the cold.

Now you know what happens when ice gets too close to a fire. You're not going to believe this story but it's really true.

So anyhow, she took in the ducks and the hare and the salmon. She put them on the little table and said, 'I'll help you off with your boots, Patrick!'

She helped Patrick off with his boots, placed them by the fire, put peats on the fire.

'Now, Patrick,' she said, 'you can smoke your pipe to your heart's content.'

And Patrick's sitting there smoking his pipe and Bridget's cutting up the salmon steaks. Oh, the fire's very hot, they were very warm, those little cottages. Patrick's sitting there, and he began to sweat. Bridget's cutting the salmon and then she looked at Patrick, for a long drip had begun to gather at the point of – didn't I tell you that Patrick had a long nose? A long drip began to gather on the point of Patrick's nose.

Then she's cutting the salmon, and she looked round and says, 'Patrick, for the love of God, man, would you take that big long drip from the front of your nose? You're making me sick!'

Now in bygone days the poor people in Ireland and Scotland, in days before handkerchiefs, they could not wipe their nose with no handkerchiefs in their pockets. They just 'wheeked' off drips with their thumb and first finger.

So, Patrick put his thumb and finger to his nose. He 'wheeked' off his nose – and threw his head in the fire! The fire was so hot it had melted the ice around his neck. And Bridget dined on salmon steaks herself that night, for Patrick – he had no head for it!

And that's the end of my story from old Ireland!

# Bag o' Lies

A long time ago Jack lived with his mother and his father in a little cottage out in the country. They werena very rich, they were kind of poor. But Jack's father had one thing he loved more than anything else. He had the fastest pony in the whole district! And he enjoyed nothing more than driving into the village and showing off. Because in these bygone days a fast pony was special. People had warned Jack's father, and his wife had warned him that some day an accident was going to happen.

So one day after visiting the village, Jack's father and his mother said goodbye to their friends. They jumped in their little gig with the fast pony and drove home. But it was a long journey, maybe three or four miles, and many bends and twists were in the road they had to take to their little croft on the hillside. And there came a storm. When there was a bolt of lightning and thunder the pony got frightened and took off. Jack's father, having had a few drinks, could not control it! The pony bolted and went over the clift. Jack's mother and father were killed.

Oh, the people in the village had warned them. But they were very sad because poor Jack was left now by himself, a ten-year-old boy. So after the funeral service and everything was settled down Jack was alone. What were they going to do with the little boy?

But then who should turn up but an old man with a wooden leg, a peg-leg, and a fisherman's bonnet while the people in the village were discussing what they were going to do with Jack!

And he pushed the people aside with his peg-leg and said, 'Look, I want to see Jack!'

And there stood little Jack among all the people. Some wanted to take him because they were friends of his father and friends of his mother.

The old man with the peg-leg stepped forward and said, 'I'm your uncle, boy. You come with me!'

Jack thought he was a strange old man – with the fisherman's bonnet and the peg-leg and the blue jacket. And he introduced himself, said he was Jack's mother's oldest brother. He had just returned from sea and heard the tragic news, but was too late to go to the funeral and everything else.

But he says, 'Laddie, you'll come with me!'

So, to make a long story short, Jack was very pleased. Because he was a jolly old fellow, was the old uncle. Jack went off to live with him to a little place he had by himself. He'd been a seaman and never married. Saving all his money, he'd bought a little croft and he had a little nest egg of money to keep himself.

'Don't worry, my lad, my son,' he said to Jack. 'You'll be all right. Your uncle will take care of you. You'll have no worries in this world.'

Jack was very happy to be with his old uncle. He liked him very much even though he'd only known him for a while. But as the days and weeks went into time, Jack came to love and respect this old uncle like nothing on this Earth. Because after the evening supper was over, what the old uncle loved to do was take Jack by the fireside, the little peat

fire, and tell him all those stories. Oh, he told him stories
galore because he'd been an old sailor! He told him stories of
his voyages into the East, stories about countries he'd visited.

And Jack thought his uncle had been telling a bit of lies at
the time, you see. But Jack said one thing and thought
another. His uncle stretched the truth sometimes, telling
Jack all those wonderful stories.

And the years passed by and Jack grew up. But Jack got
accustomed to his uncle and there was nothing more he
loved in his life than listening to his old uncle telling him
stories. By the age of twenty Jack began to mingle with the
people in the local village where his uncle lived. And naturally, a young man would get in touch in the little inn where
people gathered together. Here Jack told some of the stories
his uncle had told him!

Oh, the people were interested. The local people had love
and respect for Jack, but behind Jack's back they said, 'Hey,
Jack's a good storyteller. But doesn't he tell a pack of lies!'

And this old man says, 'Pack of lies? Jack doesn't tell a
pack of lies; Jack tells a *bag* o' lies. A real *bag o' lies*.'

But they loved Jack and they loved his stories, those he
was getting from his uncle and passing on to the people in
the village. And when Jack walked into the local pub the
young women and men, everybody expected Jack should
come and tell them the stories.

So Jack continued, till one day a messenger came through
the village on horseback. And he was crying out loud and
carrying a piece of parchment in his hand, showing it off to
everybody. The messenger dismounted at the front of the
little inn, held up the parchment, the old scroll. People gathered around. What was this message coming to the village
where Jack lived?

And the message said: THE TWENTY-FIRST BIRTHDAY OF THE

PRINCESS! Signed by the king, inviting all the storytellers and liars to come before the king: the king was celebrating the princess's birthday.

And the king himself, who was a bit of a storyteller, who loved to hear stories and tales and things like that, said there was nothing more he wanted for the princess's birthday party than to have a storytelling session. But not the kind of stories people would tell about their home life; he wanted the most fantastic stories of all! He wanted stories that were really lies. He wanted real lies. And he said he would offer a large reward to anyone who could come and tell him a story that he could not believe. But to win they must tell him something so that he, the king, would call the storyteller a liar!

But Jack wasna very interested in this.

So the people got together after the messenger had passed on to the next village. They said, 'Jack, here, Jack! Why don't you go and compete at the king's tournament and the princess's party? Why don't you tell him one of the tales you tell us? Tell the king a lie, tell the king a good lie! You have many.'

So Jack thought to himself, maybe I could. Maybe this would be a good thing for me. Now where Jack lived was only about five miles from the palace where the king was. So he went home and told his uncle:

'Uncle, uncle, I've something to tell you!' So Jack told his uncle about the messenger coming to the village and about the king wanting to hear a storyteller who could tell a lie. He said, 'Uncle, I know you've told me many lies. But, Uncle, have you told me a big enough lie that would fool the king?'

And the uncle said, 'Well, Jack, I've told you an awful lot of stories, and I'm sure some of them I've told you would fool the king.'

But Jack said, 'I'm not very happy. I don't have really a good one. Uncle, tell me another one! Tell me one I could tell the king!'

'Well, Jack,' the uncle said, 'if you want to – have you made up your mind to go? You must tell me the truth if you've made up your mind!'

Jack said, 'I want to go! It's the princess's birthday.'

But the uncle says, 'There's something you don't know, Jack. This king is a kind of conceited man, you know. There's no one in the world that the king thinks better than himself. He dresses the best, he comes before the people and says he's the best. I know about the king more than you do.'

'Well, Uncle,' Jack says, 'I want to tell the king a lie!'

He says, 'Jack, this is the lie to tell the king. You see, before you were born, Jack, I lived here with my parents. And, you see, we didna have much ground, as you know yourself, Jack. But in the East a long time ago when I was young in the ships I met an old man. And me and him got to be friends. I don't know where the man came from. He could have been Chinese, he could have been from anywhere in the world. But he and I drank together and before we parted he gave me one grain of corn.'

And Jack's listening carefully, you see!

'He gave me one grain of corn,' said the old uncle. 'So I went and took the grain of corn from him and he told me, "Take it and plant it when you go home." So my father and mother, who were your grandfather and granny, were alive at that time. I took the grain of corn home and just for the sake of fun I planted it. Out there, Jack, right in front of this little croft, I planted that grain. And the spring went by and I tended it and watered it to see what would come from it.'

And Jack's listening very careful.

And the old uncle said, 'Jack, do you know this? You've no idea what happened to that grain of corn! Within six months that grain of corn was higher than a pine tree, higher than a pine tree!'

Jack's listening.

The uncle said, 'It was into the sky sixty feet high. Then me and my father, when it was ready, we took two axes and we went out to cut it. We tried wir best to chop this one single grain down. But lo and behold the axe wouldnae take! It wouldnae even touch it. We chopped and we pushed and we chopped, but no way. So my father and me was completely exhausted. And your granny called us in for something to eat.

'So in we went for something to eat. But when we came out, lo and behold, you'll no believe this, Jack, son, the great stalk of corn was lying flat! There beside it stood the biggest hare that ever I'd seen in all my life. It was bigger than a donkey! It was crumping-crumping-crumping, eating the corn piece by piece. Me and your grandfather took wir axes and we rushed out and we managed to save the heads of the grain. But for the stalk, the hare had ate it. And then the hare was gone, it disappeared in the distance. Now,' he said, 'you go back to the king and tell the king that story!'

So, Jack being a bit of a liar thought he was going to exaggerate the truth a wee bit. He goes the next morning, takes off for the palace of the king. One by one the people came in.

'Name?'

'Jack.'

'Occupation?'

'Storyteller.'

'Are you a liar?' cried the attendant to the king.

'Well,' Jack said, 'I've told a few in my time.'

'Okay then, appear before the king!'

So they all went in to the great hall where they all sat round. And there sat the king on his throne in the middle of the floor. One by one the king called them up. And they told the king a few lies. The king listened.

He said, 'I well believe that. I well believe that,' said the king. 'I well believe that.'

And one by one off they went till it came Jack's turn. Now Jack was the last in the line. And Jack was called up before the king.

'Name?' said the king.

He says, 'Jack.'

'Occupation?'

Jack says, 'Well, I've no occupation. I just live with my uncle.'

'Storyteller? Liar?' said the king.

'Well,' Jack said, 'I've told a few in my time.'

'Well,' he said, 'you'd better tell me a few! Tell me a lie. I've called you here today because this is the birthday of my daughter the princess. And I want you to tell me a lie! Young man, if I can call you a liar I'll give you a reward. But should you fail, it's curtains for you!'

Jack said, 'There's nae problem to it.' So Jack thought.

He said: 'King, Your Majesty the King, I live with my old uncle and I'll tell you the truth. My parents were killed in an accident when my father boasted about his fast horse. And it went over the clift in a thunderstorm and it was killed. Then my old uncle came and collected me. I've lived with my old uncle ever since. He has been in many parts of the world.'

And the king said, 'But that's no a lie.'

'Well,' Jack said, 'give me time, I'm coming to the story! My uncle told me many stories in my time.'

And Jack began to tell him the story about the grain. The king said, 'I well believe that. There could be a little truth attached to that thing.' But the king said, 'And what happened to the grain?'

'Oh,' says Jack, 'you've no idea!'

Now Jack hadn't a clue what happened. But Jack being Jack thought he would tell the king what happened to the grain. His uncle had never told him. But Jack being a bit of a storyteller and a liar thought he could tell the king a story!

So, when Jack told the king about the hare coming eating the grain and eating the large corn stalk, and it falling, the king seemed to be interested, you see! And he says, 'Come, come, young man, tell me, tell me what happened to the grain?'

'Well,' thought Jack, 'I must make up something for the king.' He said, 'My grandfather and my uncle, they collected the grain after the hare had etten the stalk. And they put it in a bag. They had a secret, they had the finest grain in all the land! And they stored it away for many years. No one knew the secret of the grain.'

'I believe that,' said the king. 'But tell me, tell me, young man!' The king was getting excited:

'Tell me what happened to the grain!'

'Well,' Jack said, 'they stored it away for a long, long time. And my grandfather left it to my uncle. When I lived with my uncle he told me about it. So I said to my uncle, "Why don't we grow it?"

'"Oh never," said my uncle, "we cannae grow it, Jack. We cannae grow it!"

'But I finally convinced my uncle that we should grow the grain. So me and my uncle, we borrowed a couple of horses and ploughed the field. And we sowed the grain. And you know, Your Majesty, that grain, I watched it carefully. Kept the crows away and the birds away, out of that grain. It began to grow. I tended it carefully.'

'I believe that,' said the king.

Jack said, 'Are you calling me a liar?'

'No,' said the king, 'I'm no calling you a liar. In no way, I'm no calling you a liar!'

(Now as I told you – he was a very conceited king, this.)

He said, 'Young man, I believe it. But tell me, tell me what happened!'

'Well,' Jack says, 'the grain began to grow. And you know, Your Majesty, that grain began to grow like a pine forest. It was the highest and biggest grain – it was hanging with heavy peas of grain! And me and my uncle don't know what we're going to do with it! Oh, people came from far and wide, and they looked at it. It was like a pine forest!'

'I believe that,' said the king. But he said, 'Come tell me, what happened?'

'Well,' Jack said, 'Uncle said to me, we'll have to go get special axes made because the axes we had before wouldn't look at it. So we went to the blacksmith and got special axes made for to cut down the grain the next morning.'

The king's listening to the story. He said, 'Axes to cut down the corn, the corn stalks . . .'

But Jack said, 'We got wir axes honed and sharpened in the smiddie. And the next morning my uncle and me would attack the grain. But lo and behold – we went out to the field next morning and there was a hare, the same hare – the size of a donkey!' He said, 'Your Majesty, you wouldn't believe this! It was the biggest hare I ever saw in my life. It was bigger than a donkey.'

The king said, 'Not a hare the size of a donkey?'

Jack said, 'Are you calling me a liar?'

'No, no, young man, I'm no calling you a liar!' he said. 'Carry on with your story.'

And Jack said, 'It began to gnaw at the grain. So I said, "This is no going to happen what happened before!" I took my axe and I swung my axe at the hare. And my axe stuck in the hare's backside. And that hare got such a fright, it went round that field, round and round the grain and the stalks of grain were falling like pine trees before a storm! Then the whole thing was flat. And my uncle stood in amazement. But that wasn't the end of the story!'

The king said, 'That's hard to believe.'

'Are you calling me a liar?' said Jack.

'No, no!' he said, 'I'm no calling you a liar.'

But Jack said, 'Then the hare stopped and it began to nibble the grain. And I said, "Well if you cut it down you're no going to nibble it!" So I rushed over, pulled the axe from its backside and I kicked that hare round that field! Round and round the grain I kicked that hare. And every time I hit it a kick I kicked out a *king* from its backside! I kicked out *seven kings* out of that hare's backside. Big, strong, handsome, good-looking kings. And they stood in a row. And I'll tell you something, Your Majesty, *every one was a better king than you*!'

The king said, 'You're telling a lie – there's no one better than me!'

And Jack said, 'You give me the reward!'

So Jack got the reward from the king and he made his way home to his uncle.

And Jack's fame became far and widespread, how he had told the biggest lie to the king. Jack told all those wonderful stories to the people. The people told them to more people. And those people told them to me. I tell them to you! And that's why today they are known as 'Jack tales'.

This was told to me once by an old man away up in Aberdeenshire called Willie Lindsay. It came from the

North-East. I never heard this story in Argyll. I can give you the basic facts the way the story was told, to keep the whole story true. But they had the Doric way of telling it, using the dialect of the people.

# Hooch for Skye!

Jack stayed with his mother in this wee croft away in the west corner of Skye. And he worked around the croft here and there. So on his visits to the village he used to see this old lady at the shop, when he went to the wee shop in the store. She was always in selling eggs and things, and he fell into talk wi her one day. She asked him his name.

He said, 'Jack, they call me.'

She said, 'Where do you stay?'

'I stay away down at the end of the island wi my mother.'

She said, 'What does your mother do?'

'My mother,' he says, 'has a wee croft down there.'

'Oh aye,' she says, 'I ken your mother. I'll tell you, are ye busy?'

'No,' he said, 'my mother's wee puckle hay is cut and she's no doing very much just now.'

'Well, look,' she says, 'my old sister and me stay away down at the end o' the island, about ten miles from here. When ye go home would ye ask yer mother if she could let ye off for a couple o' days to come down and give us a wee hand wi the hay? Because we've an awful crop o' hay this year and we canna work it wirsels, seein my old sister's gettin kind o' bad in her legs.'

'Okay,' he says, 'I'll see my mother.'

She says, 'I ken yer mother fine but it's years and years since I've seen her.'

Very well, Jack goes away home wi his mother's bits o' messages. Back he goes to the wee croft, into his house and his mother says:

'Well, laddie, ye're home.'

'Aye,' Jack says, 'I'm home, Mother. But Mother, a funny thing happened to me today down at the wee store where I was down at the shop. I met an old friend of yours, she's an old woman.'

'Oh,' she says, 'I ken who ye met up wi – old Maggie. And she has an old sister Jeannie. I've never seen them for years. Jack, what was she saying to ye? Ye ken, there are a lot' o stories goes about the island about them pair.'

'Ah, Mother,' he said, 'she's a nice old woman, the nicest old woman! In fact, she wants me to come and work wi her.'

'What!' says the mother, 'gang an work wi her? Well, Jack laddie, but ye can please yersel if you want to go and work with her or no. But wi the cracks and tales that I've heard about them – they're supposed to be witches – the two o' them. And if ye're going—'

'Mother, it's for nae harm,' he says. 'The old woman only wants me to gang an' work for a couple of days wi them at the hay. Ye ken I'm no doin much here.'

'Oh well, it's up to yersel. But,' she says, 'I'm telling you, you'd better just be careful and watch what they give ye to eat, and watch what they tell ye to do. And pay attention, because they're definitely witches!'

'Ach, Mother, witches! There's nae such a thing as witches nowadays.'

Anyway, the next morning his mother makes him up a bit piece and that and he had a good bit to go, about ten mile o' a walk to the end o' the island. Away he goes, travels on and on and on; it was a lovely day, the sun was shining. He walks on, comes right down through a wee village and down to this wee croft at the side o' the shore.

Up he goes an' knocks at the door. The old woman comes out to him, 'Oh, it's you John,' she says. (She cried him John at first.) 'Come on in! I'm just getting my old sister up, old Jeannie, and giving her her breakfast.' She sits him down to the table and gives him a good breakfast. She says, 'Go round the shed there and ye'll get a scythe.' It was all the scythes they used in the olden days for cutting their hay. 'And there's a sharpening stone for sharpening it hangin in a leather case from the rafters. Ye'll get rakes and forks an' everything else ye need in the shed. I'll give ye a wee shout at dinner time.'

'All right,' says Jack.

Jack got used to this farm working, kent all about it. It was just a wee two or three acres of hay. They kept yin cow and a puckle hens, these two old sisters; they sold eggs and things. He worked away all day, cut all this hay for them. He nearly finished it.

The old sister came out and gave him a shout, 'Come on in, Jack! It's about dinner time.'

In he comes, sits down. He looks. He's never seen the other old sister before, but she's sitting at the table. He looks at her.

'Aye,' Maggie says, 'you've never met my sister, Jack. That's my sister Jeannie there. She's kind o' deaf, she'll no hear ye. She's two-three years older than me. Her legs are kind o' bad.'

'Well,' he says, 'I didna get your hay finished. I dinna ken if it's going to come on rain or no. And there's a lot –'

'Dinna worry, laddie! Dinna go home tonight!' Maggie says. 'There's plenty of room for you – ye can stay here. I'll make you a nice bed at the kitchen fire. Your mother'll ken where ye are. She'll no worry about ye.'

'All right,' says Jack.

But anyway, Jack goes away out again, works another half day. But he thought to himself, 'There's something funny about that old sister o' hers. Maggie says she's older than her, but she looks younger than her. And the way I saw her moving her feet in alow the table, there's no much wrong wi her legs! And she disna use a staff because there's no a staff lying against the table. There's something kind o' droll – I canna figure it out. But anyway, I'll mind what my mother tellt me,' so he's thinking.

But he works on again till five o'clock. The old woman gives him a shout, takes him in, gives him his supper.

Now it be coming on late in the year, the hay was late, it was about September month. The nights were coming in close. The two old women made a bed to Jack at the front o' the fire, put a big fire o' peats on. And they went away up the stairs to their bed. Jack fell asleep.

He's lying and the fire's burning down low, ken, when the peats burn down low it's just a red *grìosach*, a red fire. And he hears the feet coming down, the two old sisters coming walking down the stairs. They come right to the fire.

And old Jeannie, the one who was supposed to be crippled, says, 'He's sleeping. He'll no hear you, he's sleeping.'

Jack was lying, and he lifted the blanket a wee bit. He keeked out. This is the two old sisters, and the other ane is walking as good as you and me! They go over to the side o' the grate. And there's an oven at the side of the grate. They open the door of the oven, and one takes out a red cowl. That's a kind o' woolly bonnet or 'toorie' with a long tassel on it.

One pulls one right down over her hair. The other one

takes another one out and she pulls it over *her* hair. And they say, 'Hooch for London!'

They're gone – both of them were gone!

Jack got up, wandered around the house, lighted a lamp, searched the house upside-down outside-in, but na! Round to the byre, the cow was standing eating at the back of the byre. Right round the hayfield, he searched round the place. The two old sisters were gone, there was not a bit to be seen o' them! So he searched round and round every shed, every nook, into the henhouse, round the fields, down to the well – not a soul to be seen. The two old sisters had completely vanished. He couldn't find them anywhere.

He goes back into the house, kindles up the fire and makes himself a cup of tea.

'Man,' he says to himself, 'I doubt my mother was right. Where could those two old women go to this time o' night?' He looks at the clock. It was dead on twelve o'clock when they left, and now it was near one in the morning. Still no signs o' them. 'Ach,' he says, 'it'll no matter. I canna explain it. Maybe my mother'll tell me. But anyway, I'm going to see it through, I'm going to see what happens here. I'm no going home till I see what happens!'

But he put some more peats on the fire, went back to his bed and happed himself up. But he must have fallen asleep. He was sleeping for about a couple o' hours when he heard the door opening.

In came the first sister, and in came the second sister walking as good as me and you! Each had a bag in their hand, a leather bag. They placed the bags down on the table. And it was 'clink'; with the way they clinked – it was money that was in the bags.

So one says to the other, 'Jeannie, one for you, one for me. Put them back in the same place where we put the rest!'

'Right!' Away goes old Jeannie up the stairs with the two bags and puts them away.

Jack's lying there. He never says a word. The other old sister comes over and she stands aside the fire, she listens to see if she could hear him.

She says to herself, 'He's sleeping, he's never wakened. He disna ken the difference.' She went away up the stairs, closed the door and all was silent.

But anyway, Jack fell asleep and he must have slept on. The first thing that wakened him was the old wife giving him a shout in the morning:

'Jack, it's time to get up, seven o'clock. Rise and get your breakfast!'

'Okay,' he said, 'I'll get up.'

Jack got up, put on his clothes, had a wash. The old wife came round, gave him a good breakfast, porridge an' milk an' eggs.

She said, 'How are you this morning, Jack? Did ye sleep well last night? Anything disturb ye during the night?'

'Not a thing disturbed me during the night,' he said, 'I slept like a lamb the whole night through.'

'That's good,' she says, 'you must have been working hard.'

But anyway, Jack goes out, sharpens his scythe. Out to the field, he starts again, cuts away an' cuts away, finishes the hay. All the hay is lying out.

Old Maggie comes out, gives him a shout again, 'Come on in, Jack, it's about dinner time!'

He comes, gets his dinner, sits an' cracks to them for a long, long while. They ask him about his mother and all these things, about his croft, one thing and another until the dinner hour is up.

'Ah well,' he said, 'I'll have to go away back out an' get on with the work.'

So he went out and he started turning the hay. It was a lovely sunny day. He worked away till night-time again. He came in, had his supper. To make a long story short it came to bedtime again. The two old sisters bade him good-night.

Jack made his bed by the fire and he lay down. He looked at the clock. An old wag-at-the-wall clock was what they had on the wall: half past eleven . . . Jack's sound in bed.

But just on the chap o' twelve o'clock he hears the feet coming down the stairs again. Down they come. One says to the other, 'Is he sleeping?'

She says, 'He's sound. He must have worked hard today, but we'll make it worth his while. We'll give him a good pay.'

He's lying, Jack's lying there. He hears every word.

Up they go again to the grate, open the door of the oven. Out come the two cowls, on to their heads, 'Hooch for London!' They're off, off they go!

Same thing happened again. Jack got up, searched the house upside-down, went up the stairs. The door to their bedroom was locked.

'Now,' he said, 'I cannae break the door down – they'll ken I was up the stairs.'

He searched the house upside and down and he found this key. He tried it and the door opened. He went into their bedroom, and round the whole room. And in alow the bed he pulled out this big box, a leather-bound trunk. It was packed with wee bags, and every single bag was full o' sovereigns, gold sovereigns!

'Hmm,' he said, 'there's as much money there as would do everybody in the Isle of Skye!'

And he shoved it back in below their bed, shut the door, locked it, put the key back where he had found it, he went away back down, back to his bed, fell sound asleep. He never heard them coming back.

The next morning they came down and wakened him again. Maggie said, 'Had you a good sleep last night, Jack?'

'Oh, I slept, I was tired, dead tired. I'll finish the hay today, and—'

'Ah, but you'll have to put it up in ricks for us,' she says, 'because it will be wet lying like that. And ye ken you'll have to put it in stacks for us and do a bit o' repairs before you go away home, fencing an' that. I can employ you for a week. Your mother kens where you are so she'll no worry about you.'

He's thinking to himself now, 'Where they go tonight, I'm going with them!'

'Oh, but,' she says, 'I forgot to tell you, Jack. There's a lot o' clothes here about your size that belonged to my brother. He was just about your age when he was killed. And there's a lot o' stuff here that's nae use to me and my old sister. We'll look it out for ye and you'll take it home wi ye, it'll do for working wi'. My brother was killed.'

He says, 'What happened to your brother?'

'Oh,' she says, 'he was killed down in London. Anyway, we'll no speak about that.'

So Jack works all day, comes in, has his dinner. Works on in the afternoon again, has his supper. And he comes back in, goes to his bed.

Twelve o'clock he hears the feet coming down the stairs. He says, 'Where they're going tonight, I'm going with them!'

One old sister says to the other, 'I think he's sleeping, he's no moving.'

Over to the side of the fire they go, open the door beside the wee grate, pull out the cowls. On their heads, 'Hooch for London!'

Jack gets up out o' the bed, runs to the fire. He opens the

oven and there's one red toorie left. He pulls it on his head, 'Hooch for London!' he says. 'Hooch for London!'

He travelled through the air at about a hundred miles an hour wi this cowl on his head and the two sisters in front o' him. They circled round London and down – right through a window! And with the welt he got coming down, he didna ken any words to stop himself for landing, he was knocked out completely. See, they knew words for to cushion their blow, how to land, but he didnae. He landed after them.

When he wakened up, you know where he was lying? He was lying inside a cellar in the Royal Mint – and he was surrounded by thousands o' bags of gold sovereigns! And his toorie was gone. So were the two old sisters. They were gone. But this is where they had been going, robbing the mint every night. Two witches! But Jack searched all around . . . the mint was locked, there was no way o' him getting out – impossible!

So in the morning when the guards came down they got him sitting inside the mint. Now this was what had happened to their brother before, to the sisters' old brother. Oh, Jack was in a terrible state now – he didna ken what to do with himself!

So the guards, they asked him how he got in. But he couldn't explain. He said he didna ken how he got in. So in those days for stealing out o' the mint, the penalty was death, sentenced to death. You were hanged in an open court out in the front o' the public square.

Jack is arrested, taken out of the cellar o' the mint, taken up to the court, tried and sentenced to be hanged for robbing the Royal Mint. And so many dozens o' bags of gold that had gone a-missing – he got the blame o' the lot.

But anyway, he lay in the jail for three days, till the day he was to be hanged. He was taken out, taken up the steps, the thirteen steps to the scaffold and put on the scaffold. The hangman came, put the rope round his neck. And the minister came up to say two or three words to him before they hanged him.

The minister says to Jack, 'John, you were sentenced to death for robbing the Royal Mint. Have you anything to say before ye get hanged?'

When up the steps to the scaffold runs this old lady! She says to the hangman, 'Yes, I've got something to say!' And she placed the cowl on Jack's head, 'Hooch for Skye!' she said. The two of them were off!

And when Jack wakened up he was lying at the side of the fire back in the two old sisters' croft. As he wakens up this old sister's shouting to him, 'Jack, get up! It's time to get on wi your work!'

So Jack worked all week for the two old sisters, forgot all about it. He said, 'I must have been dreaming – that never really happened to me – I must have been dreaming. Or, was my mother right . . . did I dream or did it really happen? But anyway, I must ask them!'

At the end of the week he said to the two old sisters, 'Was I ever out o' here?'

'No,' old Maggie says, 'Jack, ye werena out o' here. You worked well. You've been the best worker ever we had here. You did everything!'

'But,' he says, 'was I no away from here, this place, during the night or anything? Did anything funny happen?'

'Na! You slept like a lamb o' God,' she says. 'You never were away from this place. Every morning we came down at breakfast time you were ay lying in your bed, and you were lying in your bed when we went to our bed at night. You've never been out of this place since you came – for a full week.'

'Ah well, that's funny . . . ach, it must hae been a dream I had. I dreamed that I landed in . . .' he tellt her the whole story. He landed in the mint and he was to be hanged till death. 'And you,' he says, 'came.'

'Ach Jack,' she says, 'you've been dreaming! The same thing happened to my poor brother. He had a dream like that too. But that's the last we ever saw o' him.'

So the old sister went away to get something for Jack, something for his breakfast. And he opened the oven and he keeked in. Inside the oven were three red toories, inside the oven!

He said, 'I wasna dreaming.' And he shut the door. She came back in.

'Well,' he says to the old sister, 'that's all your jobs finished now. I think it's about time that I went home to see how my old mother's getting on.'

'Ah but, Jack,' she says, 'my sister has made up that bundle o' clothes for you that belonged to my brother. I think they'll do ye, just the very thing. You're about his build. Wait, I'll go an' get ye your pay!'

So they gave him this big bundle of clothes to take back with him for his work. The two sisters went up the stairs and the one came down. She's carrying these two wee leather bags in her hand.

'There,' she said, 'Jack, there's your pay. And that's as much that'll keep you and your old mother for the rest o' your days.'

And Jack went away home to his mother and stayed happy for ever after.

And that's the last o' the wee story!

When I was about four years old I heard this story. My father told me the first time, and then my Uncle Duncan, a brother of my mother's, told it to me a couple of years later. The tale is a popular one among the Highland folk, but the Travellers have their own way of telling it.

# Glossary

| | |
|---|---|
| aa | all |
| afore | before |
| ahind | behind |
| ain | own |
| alow | below |
| ane | one |
| argued and bargued | disputed |
| awa | away |
| awfae | awful |
| ay | always |
| bannock | flat oatmeal cake |
| barricade, barrikit | circular tent made of tree saplings with centre fire |
| bade | resided |
| begint | began |
| beholden | held responsible |
| bene | grand |
| bing | several |
| braxy | salted sheep flesh |
| brig | bridge |
| brother | term of endearment |
| brung | brought |
| buck | tramp |
| burkers | body snatchers, who came in the middle of the night seeking people to murder for use in medical experiments |
| canna | can't |
| cane | house |
| catcht | caught |
| cheek | insolence |
| clift | cliff |
| cloot | cloth |

| | |
|---|---|
| collop | slice of meat |
| coory | snuggle, nestle |
| cowp | topple, overturn |
| crack | news, gossip |
| cratur | creature |
| crommacks | shepherds' crooks |
| cruisie | open, rushie wick lamp |
| cry | call |
| cuid | could |
| dae | do |
| dandered | walked casually |
| dee'd | died |
| deein | dying |
| didna | didn't |
| dinna | don't |
| disna | doesn't |
| dottering | stumbling feebly |
| dovering | dozing off |
| dreep | drop |
| dreich | dreary, miserable |
| droll | queer, stupid, nonsensical |
| eerie | afraid |
| etten | eaten |
| fae | from |
| feart | afraid |
| feelt | felt |
| flee | fly |
| follae | follow |
| forbyes | also |
| frae | from |
| gadgie | countryman |
| gang | go |
| gaun | going |
| gaunnae | going to |
| gie | give |
| gien | gave; given |
| gloamin | evening twilight |
| greetin terrible | utterly torturous |
| grìosach | low-burning embers |
| hae | have |
| haen | had |
| haet | thing |
| hame | home |
| hap | cover |

| | |
|---|---|
| heids | heads |
| hev | have |
| hissel(f) | himself |
| job (a wee) | urination |
| keeked | peeped |
| ken | know |
| kent | knew |
| loor | money |
| lum | chimney |
| lunaries | auras of light |
| mair | more |
| mak | make |
| messages | groceries |
| mort | woman; wife |
| nae | no |
| naebody | nobody |
| no | not |
| onybody | anybody |
| onything | anything |
| ower | over |
| oxter | the underarm |
| puckle | small amount |
| reek | smoke |
| sair | sorely |
| sarks | shirts |
| seen | saw |
| set sail | started a journey |
| shaked | shook |
| sheet apron | a large canvas sheet made into an apron |
| smiddie | blacksmith's |
| souter | cobbler |
| stotted | bounced |
| tackety | hobnailed (boots) |
| tak | take |
| tatties | potatoes |
| tellt | told |
| theirself | themselves |
| the morn | tomorrow |
| there | there's; there're |
| they | there |
| thocht | thought |
| thon | that |
| tooken | taken |
| toorie | peaked, close-fitting cap |

| two-three | a few |
| umperant | impudent |
| weans | children, wee ones |
| wi | with |
| wir | our |
| wis | was |
| wise (ye're) | unwise, not knowing |
| wonst | once |
| worl | world |
| wreft | apparition of a dead person, wraith |
| yer | your |
| ye're | you're |
| yersel | yourself |
| yese | you (*pl*) |
| yin | one |
| yinst | once |